# The Power of

Johan Bojer

**Alpha Editions**

This edition published in 2024

ISBN 9789361475177

Design and Setting By

**Alpha Editions**

www.alphaedis.com

Email - info@alphaedis.com

# Contents

# INTRODUCTION

THIS is a great book. I can have no hesitation whatever in saying that. Rarely in reading a modern novel have I felt so strong a sense of reality and so deep an impression of motive. It would be difficult to praise too highly the power and the reticence of this story.

When I compare it with other Norwegian novels, even the best and by the best-known writers, I feel that it transcends them in its high seriousness, and in the almost relentless strength with which its dominant idea is carried through. Its atmosphere is often wonderful, sometimes startling, and its structure is without any fault that has betrayed itself to me.

Of isolated scenes of beauty and pathos it has not a few, and its closeness to nature in little things fills its pages with surprises. All its characters bear the stamp of truth, and some of them are deeply impressive, especially, perhaps, that of Fru Wangen, a tragic figure of a woman, never to be forgotten as long as memory lasts.

Its theme is a noble one. That an evil act is irrevocable, that no retraction and no penitence can wipe it out; that its consequences, and the consequences of its consequences, must go on and [Pg viii]on for ever—this may not be a new thing to say, but it is a fine thing to have finely said.

I might easily dwell on the passages, and they are many, which have moved me to the highest admiration—the passages with the old pensioners, the passages (especially the last of them, at night and in bed) between the accused man and his great-hearted wife. But this would be a long task, and I am compelled to address myself to a part of my duty which may appear to be less gracious.

When I ask myself what is the effect of this book, its net result, its ultimate teaching, I am confronted by a number of questions which I find it hard to answer with enthusiasm.

This is the story of a man who signs his name as bond for a friend, and then, when the friend becomes bankrupt, denies that he has done so and accuses the friend of forgery. In the end the innocent man is committed to prison and the guilty one is banqueted by his fellow townsmen.

So far the subject of the book cannot antagonise anybody. That the right may be worsted in the battle of life and the wrong may triumph is a fact of tremendous significance, capable of treatment as great, as helpful, and as stimulating as that of the Book of Job. It is against the moral drawn by the author from this fact of life that some of us may find reason to rebel.

If I read this wonderful book aright, it says as its final word that a life of deception does not always wither up and harden the human heart, but sometimes expands and softens it; that a man may pass from lie to lie until he is convinced that he is as white as an angel, and, having betrayed himself into a belief in his innocence, that he may become generous, unselfish, and noble.

On the other hand, this book says, if I do not misunderstand it, that the sense of innocence in an innocent man may be corrupting and debasing; that to prove himself guiltless a man may make himself guilty, and that nearly every good and true impulse of the heart may be whittled away by the suspicion and abuse of the world.

I confess, though I am here to introduce this book to English readers, and do so with gladness and pride, that this is teaching of which I utterly disapprove. It conflicts with all my experience of life to think that a man may commit forgery, as Wangen does, to prove himself innocent of forgery, and that a man may become unselfish, as Norby becomes unselfish, by practising the most selfish duplicity. If I had to believe this I should also have to believe that there is no knowledge of right and wrong in the heart of man, no sense of sin, that conscience is only a juggling fiend, and that the presiding power in the world not only is not God, but the devil.

I hold it to be entirely within the right of the artist to show by what machinations of the demon of circumstance the bad man may be raised up to honour and the good man brought down to shame, but I also hold it to be the first and highest duty of the artist to show that victory may be worse than defeat, success more to be feared than failure, and that it is better to lie with the just man on his dunghill than to sit with the evil one on his throne.

That is, in my view, what great art is for—to lift us above and beyond the transient fact, the mere semblance and form of things, and show the essence of truth which life so often hides. Without it I find no function for art except that of the photographer, however faithful, the reproducer and transcriber of just what the eye can see.

All the same, I recognise the plausibility of quite other views, and I know that the opinions both on art and life of the author of this book, so far as they have revealed themselves to me, are such as receive the warm support of some of the wisest and best minds of our time.

It does not surprise me to hear that the Academy of France has lately crowned "The Power of a Lie," for both its morality and its excelling power are of the kind which at the present moment appeal most strongly to the French mind. That they will also appeal to a certain side of the Anglo-Saxon mind I confidently believe; and I am no less sure that however a reader may revolt against certain aspects of the teaching of this fine book, he will find that it stirs and touches him and makes him think.

H. C.

ISLE OF MAN, *July* 1908.

# PART I

# CHAPTER I

THE night was falling as Knut Norby drove homewards in his sledge from a meeting of the school committee. The ice on Lake Mjösen had not been safe for some little time, and he had promised his wife to go round by the high-road. But various annoyances in the course of the day had irritated the old man, and down by the craggy promontory he suddenly tightened the reins and turned off on to the ice. "It has borne others already to-day," he thought, "and there is no reason why it shouldn't bear me." The horse pricked up its ears, and stepped timidly over the rough ice; but Knut roused it with a smart touch of the whip, and the sledge bounded from hummock to hummock until it reached the smooth, shining surface of the lake.

When one annoyance follows close upon another, the feeling induced is like that of a blow falling upon a place where there is a wound already. First of all to-day, the old man had been outvoted in a school committee matter; it was against that wretched parish schoolmaster. When, in the midst of this annoyance, his son-in-law came and asked for a fresh advance upon his inheritance, it seemed to the old man like downright extortion; but when, an hour later, he heard that Wangen, the merchant, had failed, the couple of thousand krones for which he himself was liable assumed the proportions of an overwhelming calamity. "I shall soon be keeping half the parish," he thought. "People really seem to be doing their very best to rob me of my last shilling."

The horse was a long, black stallion, with a red-brown wavy mane and easy motion. The old man himself was almost hidden in a great bearskin coat with the collar turned up. The darkness was beginning to fall out on the ice, and one by one lights appeared in the farms upon the snow-covered country surrounding the bay.

"And how when my wife gets to know of this?" he thought, as the sledge-bells jingled and the ice flew from the horse's hoofs. He had put his name to Wangen's paper without her knowledge. It must have been about three or four years ago, and the guarantee was to help Wangen to obtain larger credit with a merchant in the capital. And even earlier than that, he had promised his wife not to stand surety for any one at all, for they had lost quite enough. And now? "How in the world did he manage to fool me that time?" thought Knut. But even the wisest men have their weak moments when they are good and kind. They were both in town, and Wangen had stood a good dinner at the Carl Johan Hotel. And afterwards—this happened. That had been an expensive dinner! And now with the feeling of dread at the prospect of having to stand shame-faced before his wife, and confess that he had broken his word, Norby felt a rising dislike to Wangen, who was of course to blame for it all. "He knew what he was about, that fellow, with his dinner!" And involuntarily the old man began to recall a number of bad things about Wangen; there was a kind of self-defence in feeling enraged with him.

The shadows of the fir-trees grew black, and the stars came out; while a fiery streak in the west glowed through the darkness and threw a glare upon the ice. It shone upon the plating of the harness and sledge, and cast long shadows of man and horse, that steadily kept pace with their owners. Scarcely a living being was to be seen on the desolate expanse. A solitary fisherman was visible at his hole far out, where the red reflection met the pointed shadows of the mountains; and out at the promontory might be seen a little dot of a man moving out from the land, dragging a sledge after him.

"And Herlufsen of Rud! Won't he be delighted!"

Norby, being himself of a combative disposition and hard in his dealings with others, imagined that a number of persons were always on the watch to pick a quarrel with him. If he did a good stroke of business in timber, his first feeling was one of satisfaction as he thought: "How they will envy me!" And in unfortunate transactions he did not care a rap about the money he lost; he was only troubled at the thought that it was now the turn of other people to exult.

He was now out in the middle of the ice, and had passed from the fiery reflection into the dark shadows. The horse heard sledge-bells near the shore, and without slackening its pace raised its head and neighed. "Suppose the ice were to give way!" thought the old man with a cold shiver of apprehension. His father, a wealthy old peasant, was once driving a heavy load of polished granite blocks across the lake. When the ice began to give loud reports and to bend under the weight, the old man, unwilling to throw off any of the valuable blocks in order to lighten the load, knelt down and prayed: "If only Thou wilt let me get safely to land, I'll send ten bushels of my best barley to the pastor." He got to land; but when he stood on the shore, he looked back across the ice with a chuckle, saying: "I had Him there!" And the pastor got no barley.

The sledge-bells rang out their clear, bright, silvery tones, but all the time the old man sat thinking the ice was giving way.

"If I go through, it will probably be because I didn't want to go to the sacrament next Sunday," he thought; for when he left home he had half promised his wife to call at the clerk's and give in their names for the sacrament. But at the last moment the old pagan had come to life within him, and he had driven past the clerk's house.

"It's against my conscience," he had said to himself. "I don't believe in the sacrament, scarcely in the redemption even."

There were two different men in Knut Norby. One of these had acquired ideals at school at the parsonage, in his travels, and from all kinds of books. But when, on the death of his father, Knut had had to take over the farm, he had little by little developed some traits of his father's character. The old man still seemed present among the farm-hands, in the bank-books, in the great forest, in unsettled bargains, and above all in the Norby family's standing in the country-side. It seemed natural to Knut to continue to be a part of his father, and often, when he was about to settle some new timber transaction, he would suddenly feel as if he actually were that father, and would involuntarily see with his father's eyes, use his father's artifices, and have his father's conscience. The other Knut Norby busied himself with books and with political and religious questions, whenever the first had nothing to do.

"I ought to have given in our names for that sacrament all the same," he said to himself, when he saw that he was still a long way from the shore. "It's all very well with ideas and that sort of thing; but it's not at all certain they'll be enough when we come before the judgment-seat." However, there would still be time to send word to the clerk, if only he got safely to land.

At last he reached the firm, frosty high-road, and breathed freely once more. He let the horse walk, as it was in a perspiration; but it wanted to get home to its stable, and soon broke into a trot again.

In the wood the sledge-bells sounded loud and clear. The fir-trees stretched their snow-laden branches overhead, leaving here and there a glimpse of the starry sky above.

Norby was now passing farms with lights in the windows. The largest of them, standing up on the hill, was Rud, which Norby's enemies maintained was larger than Norby's place. It was here that his great rival lived, the wealthy Mads Herlufsen of Rud.

Norby could see this farm from his own sitting-room window; and as time went on it became impossible for him to think of Herlufsen without seeing in his mind's eye his farm-buildings, the woods around, the hill behind—the whole thing like a troll with its head towards the sky; and it was all Mads Herlufsen sitting there and keeping watch upon Norby.

"And now when he hears this, how he will exult!"

His worries, which had vanished in the possibility of danger out on the ice, now returned, and he recollected having seen Wangen intoxicated on several occasions in town. "And that's the man I've helped!"

At last he turned up an avenue, at the end of which could be seen the dark mass of the Norby buildings against the fir-clad slope. In the large dwelling-house there were lights in only two or three of the windows. A large black dog came bounding towards Knut with delighted barks, leaping up in front of the horse, which snapped at it.

The stable-man came with a lantern, and held the horse while Norby, stiff with sitting still so long, got slowly out of the sledge.

Beams of light flickered across the snow from lanterns passing in and out of the doors of the cow-sheds and stables that surrounded the large farm-yard on three sides. To the left of the barn stood a separate little dwelling-house, in which lived as pensioners old disabled servants, whom Norby would not allow to become a burden upon the parish.

"Put a cloth over the horse, and don't give him water just yet," said he to the stable-man, as, whip in hand, he tramped up the steps to the house, followed by the dog.

# CHAPTER II

MARIT NORBY was proud—with the peasant women, because she looked down upon them, and with the wives of the local authorities, because she was afraid they might look down upon her.

"Oh, of course," she would say with her own peculiar smile, "we who live in the country know nothing at all!"

"You are late," she said, when Knut came in. She was sitting with her knitting in the little room between the kitchen and the large sitting-rooms. She wore a little cap upon her silvery hair, like the pastor's wife; and her face was refined and handsome, with a firm mouth and prominent chin.

"The school meeting was a lengthy one," said Knut, as he stood rubbing his hands in front of the stove.

"How did it go?" she asked, meaning the matter that she knew Knut had wanted to carry in the school committee that day.

"It went of course as badly as it could go," said Knut, turning his back to the stove. He thought he saw a sarcastic gleam in his wife's eye when he faced her, and his anger rose. Was it not enough to have had strangers worrying him to-day, without having his own people begin too? Of course she thought him a poor creature; and what would she say when she heard about Wangen?

"It seems to me you always lose, Knut," she said, sticking a knitting-needle into her hair.

"Always? No, indeed I do not!"

She knew that tone, and added adroitly, as she took the knitting-needle out again and went on knitting:

"Yes, you are always so much too good, while those who don't possess a penny, and don't pay a farthing in taxes, govern us and order us about, and we have just to say 'Thank you' and pay."

This was a healing balm, as she gave expression to the very sentiment that Norby himself was accustomed to propound.

"I suppose you've heard what has happened to Wangen," she said, smiling grimly at her knitting.

"She knows it, then, confound it!" thought the old man. He was standing in front of the stove with his hands behind him, black-bearded, bald, with his blue serge coat buttoned tightly across his broad chest. His large head drooped wearily upon his breast, and he glanced at his wife from beneath his eyebrows. He did not feel equal to any explanations this evening. He had been out in the cold for several hours, and the warmth of the house made him feel increasingly heavy and sleepy.

"Yes indeed!" he said with a yawn; "who would have thought of such a thing happening?"

She gave a little scornful laugh.

"It seems to me you have prophesied it often enough of late," she said. "But you may be glad you've had nothing to do with him."

"She doesn't know," thought Norby, with a feeling of relief.

"Ye—es," he growled in an uncertain tone of voice, his eyes dropping once more. He was not equal to either the sacrament matter or Wangen this evening.

Hearing at that moment a well-known laugh in the adjoining room, he took the opportunity of slipping out.

When he entered the next room, his daughter-in-law was sitting by a steaming bath in the middle of the floor, occupied in undressing her two-year-old son, preparatory to giving him his bath.

The old man paused at the door, and his tired face suddenly lit up.

"Who is that?" asked the fair-haired young mother, looking at the child. The boy looked at his grandfather with large, round eyes, and laughed a little shyly; but no sooner was his vest drawn over his head than he wriggled down to the floor to run to Norby. On gaining his liberty, however, he discovered the fact that he was naked, and this was even more interesting than his grandfather. He began to run backwards and forwards upon the floor, slapping his little body and laughing. Then he caught sight of his small breasts, and touched them with his fore-finger, then evaded once more the grasp of his mother, who tried to catch him, and laughed in triumph as he escaped. The old man was obliged to sit down and laugh too.

"Well, I shall go and get something good from grandfather!" said his mother; and in a twinkling the boy had climbed upon the old man's knee, and began an investigation of all his pockets, until a packet of sweets was brought to light.

The boy's name was Knut, of course. His father, Norby's eldest son, had been thrown from his sledge and killed when driving home from Lillehammer fair before the boy was born; and ever since the old man had had a horror of strong drink.

A secret worry very quickly assumes the dimensions of an actual misfortune. Just because the old man was tired and wanted to be left in peace, he felt the explanation he must have with his wife to be doubly painful. With his grandchild he always became a child himself; but this evening he could see nothing but Wangen all the time, and this irritated him. While he sat and smiled at the boy, he suddenly glanced aside, as much as to say: "Cannot you leave me in peace even here?" Wangen penetrated, as it were, into the old man's holy of holies, and Norby wanted to turn him out. He began to look upon Wangen as his enemy because he had brought dissension into his house, and because Norby had been guilty of a little deception towards his wife, which would now have to be unveiled.

"Now it's time for the bath," said the mother, taking up her boy, and while he splashed and screamed in the water, the old man stood as he always did, and laughed until the tears ran down his cheeks. But all the time he had a dim vision of Wangen's brickfields, and remembered how last autumn Wangen had instituted an eight-hours working-day. It was just like the fool! It would be a nice thing to be a farmer if such mad ideas spread and made labour conditions even worse than they were! Was it to be wondered at if such men went bankrupt? But it wasn't his fault if Wangen said more than he meant on that subject when it was a question of inducing people to stand surety for him. And the old man began to pace the floor.

"Won't grandfather say good-night to us?" said his daughter-in-law, as the old man went to the door as if about to rush out in a rage. Norby woke up. The boy was ready for bed, and was stretching out his arms towards him.

The family had supper in the little room between the kitchen and the large rooms. Since the new house had been built, they had been literally homeless, for none of them were at ease in the large, sparely-furnished rooms, and they were too much cramped for space in the little room. The hanging lamp with its glass pendants shed its light upon the tea-things and the white cloth, and a large copper kettle shone upon the old sideboard. Five people sat down to supper. There were the two daughters, Ingeborg and Laura, who sat one on each side of their father; opposite him sat his wife, with a silver chain about her neck, and a reserved expression on her face, and her daughter-in-law by her side. They still had one son living, but he was in Christiania studying philology.

"I must get you to put out my forest clothes this evening," said Norby to Ingeborg; "I must go and see to the timber-felling in the morning."

Ingeborg was the good angel of the house. Her fiancé, a young doctor, had been found dead in his bed three days before their wedding, and since then she had never been the same. Although she was not much more than five-and-twenty, her hair was sprinkled with grey, her cheeks were hollow, and her eyes had a timid, far-away look in them. She was worrying already as to what would become of her when her parents died; and in order to run no risk of being left with a bad conscience, she was constantly occupied in attending to their wants, was the first up in the morning, was always busy in the kitchen and larder, shed tears of despair when she had forgotten anything, and in spite of all this thought herself quite useless in the house.

"Do you eat as inelegantly when you are in town as you do here?" said the mother to Laura, looking sternly at her.

Laura looked a little embarrassed, and tried to throw an obstinate lock of hair off her rosy face; but she was not long in regaining her cheerfulness.

She went to school in town, and now began to talk about her old teacher and her mincing ways, her snuff-box and her inky fingers. "Dear children," she mimicked, making an exceedingly funny face, and pretending to take a pinch of snuff; "do sit still and don't give me so much trouble!" Her sister-in-law laughed, showing as she did so the absence of a front tooth; her mother could not help smiling, and even the old man glanced merrily at the lively girl.

"I will write to him to-morrow," he said to himself as he emptied his cup. "I am sure it was not more than two thousand, and if there is more——"

When at last he got into bed in his room on the first floor, he put out the light on the table by his bedside, and yawned wearily. "I'll pretend to be asleep when she comes up," he said to himself, "and then I shall be spared both sacrament and guarantee for this evening."

As he lay looking at the red glow from the half-closed draught of the stove, the door opened, and Laura crept softly in. She seated herself on the edge of her father's bed, stroked his beard two or three times, and then confided to him in a whisper that her monthly account was in terrible disorder. Her mother had not gone over it yet, but she might ask for it any day now.

"And you think you can cheat me as much as you like, do you?" said the old man from his pillows. The child withdrew her hand from his beard in some confusion, but he caught it, and as he felt how small and soft it was, he said in a sleepy voice:

"You must come into my office to-morrow, then, and we shall see!"

The girl stroked his beard once more, and laid her cheek against his, for she knew now that her deficit would be made good.

She had scarcely gone when the door opened again. The old man hastily closed his eyes; but it was Ingeborg with the clothes he had asked for upon her arm.

"Isn't some one crossing the yard with a lantern?" asked her father, seeing a light upon the blind.

"Yes, it's the dairymaid," said Ingeborg; "she's expecting a calf to-night."

And now Ingeborg too came and upon sat his bed.

"There's something I must tell you, father," she began softly. "When I was at the post-office to-day, I heard that Lawyer Basting had been declaring that you would suffer too by this failure. I didn't dare to tell mother until I had spoken to you about it."

The old man had made up his mind to be left in peace for this evening, so he said:

"Poor Basting! He's always got something or other to chatter about."

"I was sure it was untrue," said Ingeborg, rising; and after drawing the blind farther down, she quietly left the room again.

The next morning, before Norby rose, his wife asked him whether he had remembered to call at the clerk's. Upon his saying that he had not, a scene ensued, and Marit left the room, slamming the door behind her, and threatening to go to the sacrament alone.

Norby lay in bed longer than usual, for when Marit was thoroughly roused, as she was to-day, she would sometimes not utter a word for a week at a time; and then neither of them was willing to stoop low enough to be the first to bridge the gulf that separated them, and break the silence.

When at last he came down and went out into the yard, one of the men came up to him and asked with a knowing smile whether it were really true that Wangen had forged somebody's signature.

"It would be very like him if he had!" said Norby, looking up at the sky to see if it were weather for tree-felling. The man, who was busied in shovelling the snow from the road, leaned upon his spade, and looking askance at the old man, continued:

"We've heard that it's your name. He's been boasting that it's Norby himself that is surety for him; but now we hear from the house servants that it's a lie."

"It's no business of that idiot's anyhow!" thought the old man, and passed on without answering.

But on going round by the barn, where threshing was in progress, he had the same question of Wangen's forgery put to him. He still made no answer, but plunged his hand into the grain at the back of the machine, whereupon an old labourer said, as he scratched his head:

"Well, well; haven't I always said that man would see the inside of a prison some day?"

This, however, made Norby a little uneasy. "If it comes out that I have circulated a report like that," he thought, "he can make it unpleasant for me, and give people enough to talk about." He was on the point of nipping the report in the bud by explaining matters, when he caught sight, through the barn-door, of the smith going along the road with a sack upon his back.

"Has the smith been in here?" he asked.

"Yes," was the answer from several voices amidst the rustling of straw in the half-darkness.

"Then *he* knows it too!" thought Norby; "and by the evening it will be all over the parish. I must stop the smith!—Why, he was to have come and done the new sledges!" he said aloud as a pretext for rushing out and hastening down the road after the smith.

The snow-plough had not been driven along the road since the fall during the night, and it was heavy walking and still heavier running. The farther the old man ran, the angrier he became. "Here am I running like a madman," he thought, "and all because I've helped that rogue!—Ola, Ola!" he shouted, waving his hand.

But the sack on the smith's back could neither see nor hear, and the old man had to go on running. The tale must be stopped, or he might have to pay dearly for it.

At last the smith stopped because he met a man on *ski;* but before Norby came up to them the man had gone on down the hill.

"What's this I hear?" said the smith, advancing a few steps towards Norby. "That Wangen *is* a nice fellow, he is! He's fleeced me too. I've just got a bill from him for a sack of rye-flour that I paid for down!"

"It's a lie!" cried Norby, thinking of the forgery, and breathless after his run.

"A lie? No, indeed it's not; it's as true as I'm standing here!" said the smith, thinking of his flour.

But now the old man recollected the man on *ski.*

"Did you tell that man about Wangen?" he asked.

"Yes, indeed I did," said the smith. "Ah, they're bad times these!"

Norby wiped the perspiration from his face, removing his cap and wiping the crown of his head, as he turned and gazed after the man on *ski*, who was now gaily scudding down towards the fjord, raising a cloud of snow as he went. And that story was flying down with him!

Knut Norby stood there utterly helpless, gazing after him.

"It's no use now my making a fool of myself either to the smith or the men," he said to himself; "for the devil himself's gone off with the report, and I'm in a pretty fix!"

"You were calling to me, weren't you?" said the smith. "Was there anything you wanted?"

"Yes, there was!" cried the old man, turning upon him angrily. "Confound you! You've promised for months past to come and fix up my sledges; but you're a rascal, that's what you are! You owe me money and you won't pay. I'll set the bailiff upon you this very day!" And Norby set off homewards, leaving the smith standing with his sack on his back, staring after him.

"This forgery must have made him daft!" he thought, as he turned and went slowly on his way.

# CHAPTER III

AS Knut plodded homewards, he felt like a man whose hat has been blown off his head, and who cannot find out which way it has gone. He could not conceive how this rumour about Wangen's forgery had arisen, but at the same time he felt that in reality he himself was responsible for it. It was of course the women-folk who had misunderstood him yesterday evening when he was tired and wanted to be quiet. And then it had gone by way of the kitchen to the farm-hands. And by the evening the whole parish would be full of the story, for it would be quite a tit-bit to carry about. And Wangen? Of course he would take the opportunity to bring an action against Norby. He almost wished he had had a rifle in his hand, so that he could have shot the man on *ski*, who was flying along with that confounded story. If he had not existed, Norby would have had the hard task of going to his men and saying: "This is a misunderstanding about Wangen. I am actually surety for him; he has not forged my signature." But now there would be the whole parish to go to, and the thought of it made him furious.

He first turned his steps towards the kitchen entrance, to give the maid-servants a scolding, but stopped half-way across the yard. "If there's going to be any unpleasantness over this," he thought, "I shall have to bear the brunt of it after all, and I suppose I'm master in my house."

Nothing came of his projected forest excursion that day. He went instead to the stables, and threatened to discharge the stableman because a young horse was badly curried. Then he suddenly made his appearance in the barn, just when the men were taking a rest, and gave them a talking to. Finally he went into his office, and began to write dunning letters to a number of his debtors.

"I shall be fined, of course, and shall perhaps have to make a retractation in the newspaper," was his thought all the time he was writing. "This is all one gets for helping such good-for-nothings—domestic scenes, loss of money, and in addition to that you make a fool of yourself, and lose your good name!"

The door opened, and to his great astonishment Marit entered. If she was going to break the silence already, something unusual must be at the bottom of it. She had better not come too and worry him about this!

She stood erect, with both hands hanging down and her chin thrust forward, and began in a vibrating voice:

"I can see you intend to keep this from me, but I just want to ask you whether you are going to report him to the bailiff."

Knut sprang up, and stood with legs apart and his hands behind his back.

"To the bailiff?" he asked, eyeing her over the spectacles he used for writing. "No, indeed; I'm not quite crazy!"

But Marit was already incensed at his having failed her in the matter of the sacrament, and she now suspected that something else was being kept from her. She came a step nearer.

"You won't?" she cried, her voice trembling still more.

The old man began to breathe hard. Now that he was angry, her self-importance seemed both ridiculous and irritating. He would never think of confessing his misdeeds to this impertinent creature!

"What are you doing here?" he cried, throwing back his head, and glaring at her through his spectacles.

"I want you to go to the bailiff."

"Leave the room! I *will* be left in peace!"

But she laughed scornfully.

"Oh, I see you would rather pay, and pay even if your children hadn't a rag to their backs! And after this any rogue can make use of your name, and *you'll* pay! Or"—and she laughed again, and looked sharply at him— "perhaps you *have* backed his bill? Yes, I shouldn't wonder if you're guilty."

The word "guilty" sounded as if she suspected him of murder or theft. He became purple with anger, but could find no words to express his indignation. Then he caught his breath, raised his arm as if to strike, and pushed her out of the room.

Some time had elapsed when he heard sledge-bells in the yard, and looking out, he saw that it was Marit driving off. Oh, indeed! They were beginning to take the horses out of the stable without asking his leave, were they? "The next thing she'll take will be my breeches," he said to himself, beginning to pace the floor, as his habit was when angry.

A little later he heard the bells returning. He did not look out, but lay down upon the leather sofa and closed his eyes. Soon after he heard the well-known steps in the passage, the door opened, and Marit entered; but the old man lay still with his eyes closed.

She began at once, while she untied the strings of her bonnet.

"I know quite well you're man enough to order me to leave the room once more; but as you're not man enough to look after your own affairs, I shall have to do it for you; and as sure as I'm mistress in this house, this shall not pass. So now I've been to the bailiff."

Knut rose slowly, pushing the rug aside. He gazed at her, opened his mouth and gazed. At last he passed his hand through his beard, and then over his bald head, and said in an uncomfortably ordinary tone of voice:

"Oh, have you been to the bailiff, Marit?"

"Yes! When there are no men on the farm, the women have to go out to work," she said. "I didn't come quite empty-handed when I became mistress at Norby, and I didn't mean to let you give my share to tramps and beggars."

Knut turned pale, but once more passed his hand over his bald crown and through his beard, and tried to laugh. She could hardly have wounded the capable Knut Norby more deeply, for he had about doubled their fortune.

Marit now deemed it wisest to withdraw, but she closed the door slowly behind her, and walked with slow firm step. Knut remained sitting, and again passed his hand over his head two or three times. For the first time in his life Norby thought of going after his wife and thrashing her, for domestic peace was at an end anyhow.

He rose and began to wander about with his thumbs in the armholes of his waistcoat. Now and again he stood still as if to make quite certain whether this was not a dream from which he might awake. But there stood the outhouses right enough, painted red, and a magpie let itself slip down the sloping roof, and left a furrow in the snow; and there hung Johan Sverdrup over the writing-table, and he himself stood here and still had his forest clothes on. No, it must be true after all that his wife had been to the bailiff—with this——

The floor seemed to become insecure beneath his feet, the office became too small, and he had to go into the large corner room, where he began to walk about with his hands in his pockets. Here there was mahogany furniture and there were large gilt-framed mirrors and other splendours, but now it seemed to Norby as if they were his no longer. He stood still again and again to wonder: "Is it you, Norby, or is it not?"

He stood at the window in the white light reflected from the snow, and looked out at the half-buried garden. But it was not the trees he saw. He saw himself being driven down the hill by the bailiff on his way to prison for having brought a false accusation.

He turned suddenly round, and went resolutely towards the door, but stopped with his hand on the handle. He felt that it was utterly impossible to go to his wife now and tell her the truth, in the first place because he felt more inclined to thrash her, and in the second because he did not know how she would take such a communication. She would perhaps only faint with rage at having run like a fool to the village, but she might also do something worse.

He mounted the stairs to his room in order to change his clothes. He must go to the bailiff. But when his trousers were off, and he was about to pull on his blue serge ones, his hands dropped and he sighed heavily.

"Now isn't all this a sin and a shame!" he thought. "First I help the man out of kindness, then I have to pay up, then there's a row in the house, and then I run about and make a fool of myself. And now I was actually going off to hold up my wife to the ridicule of the whole parish! No, that is really going too far!"

He remained sitting with the new trousers in his hand. Yesterday's unpleasant picture of Wangen had become still more unpleasant now, for in reality he was to blame for all this to-day too. And for that man he was ready to——! The old man suddenly threw down the serge trousers, and drew on the old ones; for if he did withdraw his accusation from the bailiff, he would still have to answer for the report. And go to Wangen and eat humble pie? To ask pardon of that man? Never! Never would he do it!

No, there must be some back way out of this. He would think it over.

Knut Norby suddenly found himself in a misfortune for which he himself was not exactly to blame, but for which he had to bear the responsibility. He did not therefore feel the responsibility to be quite so heavy as it otherwise would have been. All the misery that had come upon his house to-day was thanks to his kindness in helping that fellow. It was Wangen's fault altogether.

When the old man was sitting in the little room at dusk, he heard little Knut laughing in the next room, and rose to go in to him, but stopped at the door. He was not equal to seeing little Knut to-day.

"Perhaps he had a hand in bringing your father to such a bad end too," he said to himself, thinking of the child. At any rate, Wangen was at Lillehammer fair that time.

One day went by, and then another. The old man was on thorns. But every time he thought of changing his clothes and going to the bailiff, he half unconsciously began to conjure up a picture of Wangen, to remember bad things about him, to place him in a ridiculous or an odious light, to impute to him all kinds of repulsive failings; and this gave him fresh courage to put off going, and he felt it more and more impossible that he should humble himself to such a man.

And suppose that Wangen was to blame for his son's death? Although this possibility made the old man sick with anger, he was still uneasy in his mind. The witness, Jörgen Haarstad, was dead, it was true; but Knut Norby would not disown his signature. There must be some back way out of it.

# CHAPTER IV

HENRY WANGEN descended from the snow-covered train from Christiania, and with his bag in his hand hurried homewards. He exchanged greetings with no one. His failure would ruin half the parish, and he knew that people stood and looked after him as they would after a rogue they would like to thrash.

He was a man of about five-and-thirty, tall and spare, with a reddish beard and a refined, youthful face. But he walked like an old man. His going humbly from one merchant to another in Christiania had been in vain; and he dreaded going home, because his wife must at last be told the truth.

Henry Wangen was the son of a magistrate who had misappropriated the public funds. He had tried many occupations, but was an agriculturist when he married the daughter of a wealthy fanner. Her father, who had long opposed the marriage, made it a condition that she should have the control of her own property. But when Wangen started the brickfields, he not only obtained his wife's confidence and money, but he was so eloquent and enthusiastic that he also induced her father and brother, and many others, to entrust him with their money. And now?

When he came to the end of the bridge, where a number of cottages are dotted over the hill, he met a bent figure in a faded overcoat and fur cap, with a toothless mouth and a pair of gold spectacles upon a prominent red nose. Wangen stopped, opened his bag, and took out a bottle wrapped in paper. It was a commission he had had in town. The man with the spectacles smiled at the bottle as at something very precious, and put it under his arm.

"I say!" he said with a smile, "I've got a little piece of news for you."

But Wangen was gone. He was thinking of his wife, who was expecting their fourth child. Could she bear what he had to tell her?

The other followed him, however, and took hold of his arm.

"Oh, but you must wait and hear the news!" he said, and laughed a little spitefully. "Come in a moment, and taste the purchase."

"No, I can't just now," said Wangen, hurrying on. Wangen had unfortunately more than once allowed himself to be tempted by this inebriate consul from Christiania, whose relations boarded him here in the country; but now he was determined to be thoroughly sober when he got home. The elder man still hung upon his arm, however, and spoke so persuasively that he at length allowed himself to be drawn into his little house.

At the window of the low room they entered, which smelt of whisky and tobacco, sat a lean, tailor-like figure, playing patience. This was the third member of the whisky-drinking trio, an old lawyer, crippled with rheumatism, and long since past work. He went by the name of "the late future prime minister."

"Sit down!" said the consul, but Wangen remained standing with his bag in his hand.

"Shall we have a game at cards?" said the man at the window, smiling in his white beard.

"Hold your tongue!" said the consul, busying himself with the rinsing of two glasses. "We're first going to have a glass of three-stars."

"No, I won't have any!" said Wangen. "But what was it that I positively must hear?"

"Just you sit down, my boy!" said the consul, chuckling as he held up a glass to the light. "Upon my word, the world is worse than I thought."

This meant a good deal, for the consul was not accustomed to judge people leniently.

"What is it?" said Wangen. "Has anything happened to my wife?"

The consul placed the glasses on the table, and fixed his little, venomous eyes upon Wangen, while his red nose wrinkled in a smile.

"Oh well, so many things happen," he said. "Now for instance, what is your opinion of the great man at Norby?"

"Norby? I really don't know. I've got enough to do to look after myself. But I must go."

"Wait!" said the consul. "Norby must have a spite against you, for, to tell the truth, he means to get you sent to prison because you have forged his signature."

The prime minister looked up from his patience, and tried to see by Wangen's face whether he should laugh or not.

There was a short pause, during which the consul enjoyed the situation and continued to gaze at Wangen through his spectacles.

Wangen broke into a laugh, and involuntarily stretched out his hand for the filled glass.

"Your health!" he said. "That's not a bad story!"

"You don't believe it, perhaps? Upon my word it's true, old chap! Ask the prime minister!"

The late future prime minister nodded.

Wangen looked from the one to the other.

"What's all this nonsense you're talking?" he said. He did not believe it yet.

"You may well say so," said the consul with a venomous smile. "It's a delightful world we live in!"

"Has any one been to tell my wife?" Wangen's voice trembled, and he turned pale. He reached out his hand for his bag.

"Yes, she's had a visitor," said the consul, with his most venomous glance.

"The bailiff?"

"Yes."

"Because—because I've committed forgery?"

"Exactly." The consul was enjoying the situation to such an extent that he forgot to empty his glass.

Wangen had emptied his, and now held it out for more.

"Your health!" he said. "If this is true, then by Jove it'll be Norby and not me to go to prison!" And with that he buttoned up his coat and hurried to the door.

# CHAPTER V

IT sometimes happens that in the even current of our lives we suddenly meet with an obstacle that compels us to pause and consider. To Henry Wangen his failure was such an obstacle as this. As he sat in the train on his way home from town, with unavoidable ruin staring him in the face, he was nearly passing sentence of death upon himself. He saw that this failure, which brought misfortune to so many, was due to his own incapacity and recklessness. It was terrible, but it was true.

"This is a consequence of never having taken the trouble to acquire thorough knowledge," he thought. "And if I hadn't so often sat drinking far into the night at the consul's, I should have had more judgment in my business the next day." Every drowsy or lazy moment in which a determination was taken now seemed to him to have come to life in the form of a starving, despairing family. "There! There!"

And during these moments of calm justice towards himself, he saw one thing that impressed him more than any other, namely, that his kindness of heart had really been a greater enemy to him than drink; for he had always contented himself with the knowledge that he meant well. And he did mean it all so well, and sheltered by this good intention, he had done the most thoughtless acts, and always with a good conscience; for good faith was always ready to excuse the blackest lies and raise them into the light of truth.

And now? Reality had no use for good faith; it demanded more.

While the train rolled on, he also saw how his pet idea for the improvement of the conditions of the working-man, an eight-hours' working-day, had also helped in the ruin. So it was not only necessary to have benevolent ideas in this world; they must be such as did not bring misfortune upon those they were intended to help, as they had done in this case.

He was filled with a dull rage against himself, and swore that he would not rest until he had paid back to them all that he had wheedled out of them. He swore not to touch strong drink again. He was fully aware that this was not enough. He would never, never be able to make up for the suffering he had brought upon so many.

And his wife, who had put such confidence in him? He felt as if he could have taken himself by the throat and called himself a scoundrel.

He was now on his way home from the consul's after having heard the "news." Strange to say, his mind had become more composed. He did not hang his head any longer. He walked more easily. He did not know himself how it came about, but he was not quite so afraid of going home to his wife and confessing the truth.

When he came in sight of his house, which lay a little to the left of the dark mass of the brick-kilns, he saw a light in a single window. He remembered his wife's condition and the bailiff's visit. "Poor Karen!" he thought; "perhaps she was at home, alone too." And a flood of anger filled his heart, anger this time not against himself, but against Norby. "Is he quite mad? What does he mean by this?" It was a relief to be able to turn his indignation against others than himself.

When he entered the dining-room where he had seen the light, he found his young wife sitting by a small lamp. She rose mechanically. He saw at once that the children were in bed, and the supper was laid and waiting for him. How cosy and peaceful it was! But in the middle of this peace she stood pale and frightened, gazing at him as if she would say: "Tell me quickly, is it true?"

She was a tall, stately woman, not yet thirty years of age. She was dressed in a loose-fitting grey dress, and her wealth of fair hair was set like a crown upon her head. Her long eyelashes gave a depth and brightness to her eyes. Her face was in the shadow of the lamp-shade, as she stood leaning upon the back of a chair, motionless, impatient and anxious.

"I know all!" he said abruptly, stooping to put down his bag; and even before he raised himself again, he heard her drop into a chair and burst into tears.

"I thought I should have gone out of my mind!" she sobbed.

He stood looking at her. She did not come up to him and throw her arms about his neck. Did she really suspect him? His indignation and pain at this again felt like a relief; for in this he was innocent at any rate; he could defend himself here with a good conscience.

He went up to her, and laid his hand on her shoulder.

"Karen!" he said, "do you believe it?"

There was a pause, during which he grew more and more anxious. At last she raised her hand and placed it in his. He clasped it; it was so thin and helpless, and so warm, and it seemed to give him all her confidence. It is true that during the last few days she had often reproached him, and had mercilessly demanded from him the return of her money; but this was beyond ordinary limits, and made everything else seem small, and now she clung to him confidingly.

In a little while she pointed to the supper-table and whispered: "Won't you have supper?" And she rose slowly and went to the stove for the tea-pot. "Would you like me to light the big lamp?" she asked gently.

"No, dear," he said, seating himself at the table, and beginning to eat, more for the purpose of removing the smell of whisky than of satisfying any hunger. He noticed that there was a half-bottle of beer upon the table, and this positively agitated him. They could not afford to drink beer now, but perhaps she had found this last bottle in some box, and in spite of her own troubles, had not forgotten to put it on the table when she expected him.

"Have you had supper?" he asked, as she did not come to table.

"No, thank you," she said; "I don't think I can eat anything."

"Oh yes, Karen," he said; "Sören will want his supper, you know."

This little joke seemed so strange in their present gloomy mood. For Sören was their secret pet-name for the little one that was still unborn. And now, when the father said this, it was as though a little bridge of gold had been thrown between them, and she could not help looking brightly up at him and smiling.

That smile seemed to light up the room. It relieved them both, and they were now able to talk quietly about this affair with Norby.

"Can you imagine what has made him do it?" she said, as she poured herself out a cup of tea.

He felt her eyes upon him, and this time he could raise his head and meet them.

"Well, it must come to light some day. It is either a misunderstanding, or——"

"Or?" she questioned.

While he was seeking for probable reasons, he felt at the same time an ill-defined anxiety lest it should only be a misunderstanding. A star seemed to have risen in the firmament of his consciousness, and pointed to an inquiry, acquittal, and reparation. Half unconsciously he felt that this would be salvation, not only as regarded this accusation, but also all others.

"Norby is one of those men of whom you never can make anything," he answered. "It is quite possible that the couple of thousand now in question have quite robbed him of his wits."

She raised her eyes, and her glance said: "Two thousand? There too!" And she almost imperceptibly shook her head.

With an involuntary anxiety lest she should attach too much importance to this side of the question, he continued:

"He's a great idiot anyhow; for he must surely understand that as there's a witness, he can't get out of it."

As they talked, and he was able to occupy himself with his innocence in the matter, his tranquillity of mind increased, and things looked easier and brighter. And he carried her along with him. She had quite forgotten to ask how he had got on in town, and whether he could save her money. An event had taken place in the house which swept everything else into the background.

"How did you get on in town to-day?" she asked at length.

And he could answer frankly now: "Karen dear, the worst is about your money——" He could get no further, his voice grew husky. Instead of being afraid and in despair, he now felt so certain of forgiveness that he could safely be distressed.

He was quite right. She did not spring up. She did not call him to account for all his false representations. She bowed her head; she still had a vision of the bailiff before her eyes, and she answered with a sigh:

"Well, well—so long as you are innocent in this——"

"Don't say that, Karen!" he said with tears in his eyes. "I feel that I have so much to answer for both to you and——"

"Oh, it may turn out all right in the end," she said, her face turned towards the lamp. "So long as one doesn't lose one's honour."

So that was over. He had not this confession to dread any longer; but he had never dreamt it would have been got through so easily.

"What is it, though?" he thought, as he rose from the table. He felt as if it were his duty to be unhappy, and now he could not. He kept his eyes all the time fixed upon his innocence in this one matter, and this feeling of innocence was like a lamp that suddenly shone upon his darkness; it illuminated everything, softened everything, so that the remorse and despair he had felt in the train, all that had chafed and wounded him earlier in the day, melted away into far-off, shapeless mist.

He had to go into the bedroom to look at the children, and he sat down on the edge of the bed in which the two little girls slept. In the train he had felt himself unworthy to bring children into the world, but now he was once more happy in being a father.

"How long do you think we shall be able to stay here?" she asked, when he came in again. "Do you think we shall have to move before I am laid up?"

It sounded so unusually resigned.

"No," he said; "certainly not."

They walked through the rooms, he carrying the lamp. They seemed to have a mutual feeling that it would soon all be taken from them, and they be left homeless and empty-handed. They paused in front of various things—a mirror, a rug, a picture—and looked at them, his disengaged arm round her waist, as if to support her.

"Do you know," she said with a little sigh, "when my confinement is over I'm going to try to do without a servant."

"Oh," said he, "there will be no sense in that."

"Yes, but, Henry, have you considered what we're going to live upon?"

He recollected a vow he had made in the train, to put his hand to any sort of work, if only she, to whom he owed so much, could live free from care. But he said nothing about it now. This feeling of innocence gave him an involuntary pride, and he contented himself with saying:

"Let's hope I shall yet be able to arrange a composition."

He drew her closer to him, as if to have her with him in this faint hope; and she leaned against him, with her fair head resting upon his shoulder, now that she felt sure that he was innocent of this crime, before which everything else dwindled into easily surmountable trifles.

The maid was out. They were alone in the house, and the stillness made them talk in undertones. She grew tired of standing, and sank down upon a sofa; and he seated himself beside her, when he had placed the lamp upon a table close by.

They sat in silence, gazing vacantly at the piano. The little lamp threw a pale light about them, while the furniture in the rest of the room was lost in the darkness.

"Father came while the bailiff was here," she said at last, looking straight before her.

"How did he take it?"

"Every one will believe you're guilty," she said. "And Norby is powerful. Father is coming again to-morrow. You'd promised to bring him from town the last ten thousand krones he got for you."

Wangen's head drooped. A vision of her father, with his white hair and red, watery eyes, came before him. What should he say to the old man to-morrow, now that everything was lost?

"And the widow from Thorstad has been here," she went on. "You had promised her half as soon as you came from town."

Wangen still stared into the shadow by the piano. He was afraid she would ask him if he had the money.

"It is worst for the working-men," she continued, "who are now quite destitute, and cannot get credit anywhere. And in the middle of winter too!" She was on the verge of tears.

Perhaps they too would be coming in the morning to ask about what he had promised them. In the half-darkness Wangen could see before him the old man with the red, watery eyes, the widow whose fortune he had wasted, the work-people—all of them. They would all come in the morning, and call him to account.

He turned cold at the thought, and the same dark accusation he had brought against himself in the train appeared once more, while he felt his clear innocence of forgery to be valueless; it grew fainter, like a lantern on the point of going out, leaving him in a darkness where the crushing sense of responsibility brought him to despair, where remorse fastened upon him with innumerable hands, and where he must eternally and inexorably remain a prisoner and be tortured with the pains of hell.

He rose suddenly. "Let's go into the other room," he said, raising his shoulders; "it's so cold here."

In the dining-room he placed the lamp on the table, and stood a moment gazing at it.

"When I think about it," he said at last, "I can after all understand why Norby wants to injure me."

"Can you?" she said eagerly.

He continued to stand motionless in the same position.

"Yes," he said; "that man is both jealous of his honour and revengeful. He wasn't made chairman of the parish last time either, and I expect he thinks it's my fault."

"Good heavens!" she sighed.

As he stood there, he could see in his mind's eye Norby with his cherished grudge, sitting in his house like a wicked ogre, ready to burst with a desire for revenge, and this distorted picture strengthened Wangen's feeling of innocence, which now seemed like a kind of thread upon which he hung, and which must not break.

He heard his wife say good-night, but he still stood there. When at last he went into the bedroom, she was standing half-undressed in front of the looking-glass, doing up her thick hair for the night in a long plait.

"And what's more," he said softly, gazing as if at a dawning salvation, "I understand now why Norby managed to frustrate the intention of building the church of brick. The brickfields, do you see, shouldn't make anything out of it. Norby wanted to provide the timber."

He began to walk up and down, and then stopped again. "And now I understand too," he went on, "how it is that so many customers have left me lately. The brickfields were to be removed out of the way of the large forest-owners here."

"Do you really think so?" she exclaimed, turning from the glass and looking at him, half in horror that people could be so wicked, half in gladness that the decline in the brickfields business was not wholly his fault.

The wind began to howl in the great factory chimneys. A door up in the loft opened and shut with a bang so that the house shook.

"Oh, would you mind?" she said. "That door has been banging ever since the girl went out, but I didn't venture on the stairs. Will you?"

He went, and on coming down again he said:

"And this normal working-day—it has frightened the rich big-wigs too. Yes, now I begin to understand."

And each time he exhumed a fresh probability of a conspiracy against him, it lifted a fresh burden from his own shoulders; so he dug again and again, half in anxiety that he should not be able to find enough.

While Fru Wangen stood in her night-dress by the bed, winding up her watch for the night, he came and laid his arm round her shoulders, and said with some emotion:

"So now, Karen, it can be explained why they have begun to lose confidence in me in town, and I am hardly likely to be allowed to compound. The rumour of a crime will knock that on the head."

"Poor Henry!" she said, and hanging her watch in its place, she turned and threw her arms about his neck. "I'm afraid I've misjudged you, Henry! Can you forgive me?"

He was touched, and folded her in a close embrace, feeling as he did so the warmth of her body through her nightdress. They stood thus silent, her head upon his shoulder, both seeing the same persecution and injustice, feeling themselves united in the same innocence, and finding warmth in their mutual need of standing together.

And now when he thought of her money, it no longer seemed to be his fault; the blame was transferred to those in whose way the brick-kilns had lain. And he thought of her old, ruined father, and he no longer dreaded his coming in the morning. The widow, the workmen's families passed before his mind's eye, but they no longer accused him. He felt sympathy for them, and indignation on their account; but now the indignation was turned against others, not against himself.

"Aren't you coming to bed?" she asked.

"Oh, wait a little!" he said, still standing as before.

"Yes, but I'm getting cold, Henry."

He was actually afraid of letting her go, as if she were the happy conscience he had now built up, which felt like a deliverance from something terrible.

"I think I'll go out for a little," he said at last. "I shan't be able to sleep anyhow."

"Don't be out too long!" she said. "Remember I'm lying here alone."

Of course he would not be long. But she was anxious nevertheless; for he was always "only going out for a little" when it ended at the consul's, and he came home a little unsteady in his gait.

Wangen set out with his hands deep in the pockets of his coat. The hard snow creaked beneath his feet, and above the snowy hills and dark ridges was spread a wide, brilliant, starry sky.

"Thank goodness!" thought Wangen, "that eight-hours' working-day probably has nothing to do with the failure." And he involuntarily felt as if a lost ideal had been regained, so that he had a beloved, bright idea for the future to believe in. From this his thoughts passed insensibly to Norby and the other rich men, who sat brooding over their money-bags, suspicious of everything new, fearful of everything, averse to all improvement of the condition of the lower classes.

"They managed to quash it this time," he thought; "but there will be a next time."

He walked on until he found himself outside the consul's house. A light was still burning in the sitting-room. A good impulse took him by the button-hole and said: "Remember your vow in the train!" But there are times when we feel ourselves so morally well-to-do that we think nothing of flinging away a halfpenny. Wangen must have some one to talk to now, and he would only stay a quarter of an hour.

"Why, dear me! Aren't you arrested yet?" said the consul, who was sitting in his dressing-gown, stirring a freshly-made toddy.

And they sat with the bottle between them, and discussed the matter very thoroughly. Wangen talked himself into more guesses, suspected more rich men, one after another, of being in the conspiracy, and was lavish in his use of forcible expressions about them all. The consul encouraged him with little spiteful remarks, and made numerous mental notes. To-morrow he would go for a walk.

They emptied the bottle between them, and when Wangen went home a little after midnight, he stumbled every now and then over his own boots.

"Poor consul!" he thought, dreading going home; "he has had a hard life, and needs a little sympathy and appreciation."

When he staggered into the bedroom, his wife awoke with a cry of terror.

His head was heavy next morning; he was ashamed to meet his wife, and again began to dread meeting those who were to come to him that day.

By clinging, however, to his innocence in the one matter, he very soon succeeded in regaining his self-confidence; and when, later in the day, he had to go to the station, he was no longer afraid of meeting people. He began to entertain a dim idea of giving a lecture to the workmen, and explaining to them the true cause of their common ruin.

As he went homewards, the sun was shining upon the wide, snow-covered fields, and dazzled his eyes. There stood the dead factory-buildings with their tall chimneys, seeming to cry to heaven; but it was not with him they had to do. Yesterday in the train he had thought that his own house was too luxurious, and the factory buildings too large and expensive; but now he looked at everything with different eyes. He knew in his own heart that he had built these works in an honest belief in the future of this industry in the district; and a banner of innocence waved over both the works and the house.

# CHAPTER VI

DAY after day passed, and Norby had not yet recalled his declaration. A notice of the forgery had already appeared in the newspaper, and the more the story spread and grew, the more humiliating it seemed to Norby it would be to retract; and the longer he put off, the more the dread of humiliation grew, and the more powerless did he feel to stoop and take the consequences.

It would in fact be deliberately to make himself out a dishonourable man. Was that too to be the thanks he got for having in his kindness of heart helped Wangen?

His enemies? They would rejoice as long as he lived. And the parish? An avalanche of ridicule would descend upon him, and he would always feel as if he were standing in the pillory to be the laughing-stock of every one.

In Norby's eyes the parish was something of indefinite size, which only paid attention to what he did. It was his parish, and he saw it especially when he lay with closed eyes. The woods and farms and hills and rivers were the same, but the people were of two kinds—those who praised him, and those who spoke evil of him. There lived no others in the parish. The first he looked upon as honourable, worthy people, the second as his enemies whom he should certainly not forget. And now? He was quite sure that now people did nothing but talk about this affair. Heads were put in at doors, voices called across back-yards: Have you heard it? He saw people bustling up paths, flying off on *ski*, writing letters to other villages and towns: Have you heard it?

And if he now gave his wife away to this same parish, there would be further excitement; it made him angry to think of it.

But now people began to come to the old man and talk about the matter. What was he to say? He must say something. At first he tried to get away from the subject, but afterwards he was afraid that he might have betrayed himself. "I am an idiot," he thought. "It won't make it any worse than it is already if I say it until I can find a way out." And at last the day came when he said it in so many words, half in impatience to be left alone.

When the stranger went away, the old man stood at the window looking after him with a feeling similar to that with which he had looked after the man on *ski* that day. This man would tell it to others. He had said something that he could never recall.

He felt now that the way to the bailiff was closed. He must keep it up for the present. And henceforward, every time he repeated the bitter falsehood, he felt bound to say it once more in order to make it consistent. But he always stood, as it were, and looked after this dangerous lie, which branched out from his own tongue, wandered about the parish, and grew every day like a spectre that would one day turn against him. And yet he was obliged to help the spectre to grow still more, for, like the lion-tamer who dares not turn his back on the lion, he must not waver, must not show fear, and there was nothing to be done but to stick to the story.

During the dark, snow-laden, winter days, the old man tramped about the yard, went in at one outhouse door, came out of another, scolded a little here and there, and imagined he was busy, which he was not. When he knew he was not observed he would stand and stare at his boots, then shake his head and say: "If it only hadn't been Herlufsen!"

But there sat the house like the troll with its head up to the sky, and called across the valley, jibing and mocking as it always did when Norby was in trouble: "How are you, Norby? Do you feel bad?"

"Poor father!" said Ingeborg to her mother in the kitchen. "He begins to look so pale and wretched; he can't possibly be well."

"No," said her mother; "I suppose it's this affair that is telling upon him. Of course it can't be very pleasant, but it isn't our fault. Wangen has himself to thank for it."

Ingeborg became doubly zealous in her attentions to her father the more depressed he seemed to be. How touched she was at his taking the matter so much to heart! People could see now how good her father was! She had always known that he was the best man in the world.

But how frightened the poor girl was the day she heard that Wangen had said that it was Norby, and not himself, who would go to prison. Up to that time she had had a certain amount of sympathy with Wangen, because he was guilty; but now he became a dreadful man in her eyes. And suppose he succeeded in bringing trouble upon her father! She dared not mention it to her mother, and as there was no one to whom she could confide her anxiety, it grew larger and larger, and began to keep her awake at night.

It was now, however, that she sought comfort of God, and every night prayed long, fervent prayers; but she knew that if her prayers were to be answered, she must make herself worthy to pray. She thought too that as she succeeded in overcoming the powers of evil in herself, she noticed that her prayers seemed to receive comforting answers; and little by little she began to see her father surrounded by the powers of goodness, who would protect him. How happy she was! Wangen could not hurt him now; he might try if he liked, but it would be of no use!

From that day the weary, sad girl began to go about with a brighter face and lighter step, as if she had a secret joy glowing within her.

The disagreement between Norby and his wife was over; but it had never been so impossible to tell her the rights of the case as it was now.

One day, about the middle of the week, the old man drove Laura in the double sledge to the station, as she was going back to town to continue school. It was a frosty day with cloudless sky and glittering stretches of snow. The sledge-runners creaked upon the hard snowy road. The old man sat in his fur coat, and glanced now and then at his daughter. He had never seen her so pretty as she was to-day. The frost had put such a colour into her young cheeks, and made her eyes so clear and blue; and the oftener she turned those eyes upon him while she talked and laughed the more ashamed did he feel of no longer deserving this child's confidence.

"You must write to us a little oftener than you generally do," he said, looking straight before him at the horse. "We should like to know if anything happens to you."

When he said good-bye at the station, while the engine stood snorting preparatory to the departure of the train, he had a great desire to kiss her on the forehead; but caresses were not in Norby's line, and he contented himself with slipping some extra money into her hand.

"You must buy something with that," he said. That was the kiss.

When he drove home again in the sledge, he felt as though he were alone in the world. And who could tell what evil he was now driving towards, as he went home to Norby?

When he arrived there, Marit met him at the outer door.

"You've actually gone and forgotten that declaration again," she said, referring to a written declaration to the merchant with whom Wangen had deposited his guarantee document.

"Where's the hurry?" murmured the old man as he took off his fur coat.

"It's been lying here for a week now, and yesterday he telephoned to ask what had become of it."

Norby went slowly into his office where the declaration lay written out. But though he had now spoken about Wangen's forgery to all sorts of people, it was quite another thing to have to put his name to it.

Marit had followed him, and she stood waiting at the door.

"Must it be done now?" said the old man, slowly raising his eyes to hers as he fumbled for his spectacle-case.

"I am going to the post-office, and I'll take it with me."

Marit felt herself the motive-power in this affair. She feared that behind her back he might be prevailed upon to pull down what she had built up.

He dipped his pen in the ink, but then paused and sat gazing at Johan Sverdrup's portrait.

"It's a bad business, this," he said, with his eyes upon the portrait.

"Yes!" she said, shrugging her shoulders. "You must protect yourself and your belongings while there's law and justice in the land."

"Yes, yes," sighed the old man. And again he saw the spectre that grew and grew, and would fall down upon him on the day he turned round; and slowly he signed his name, Knut O. Norby.

When his wife had left the house he was once more standing and looking after an action that was set in motion and could not be overtaken. The thing was done now; he had put his name to a false declaration. The name Knut O. Norby would henceforth not be so well esteemed as formerly.

"No, I must find some work to do," he thought, shaking himself. "Perhaps that'll cheer me up."

But feeling rather tired, for he had not slept much the night before, he lay down upon the leather sofa and closed his eyes for a moment, feeling as though he should not be able to get up for ever so long.

What made him uncomfortable was that he now always had a vision of Wangen before him. Ever since the day when he had set Wangen in an ugly light in order to have an excuse for not going to the bailiff, the man seemed burnt into his consciousness. He began to meet him everywhere, and to see him in every one he talked to. He saw him now, and sprang up and out, harnessed a horse, and drove to the forest to look at the timber-driving.

He heard the crash of the logs far in among the hills, and was not long in getting there. Some great trunks had been driven out to the road, and a load was just coming to the top of the steep hill where a slide had been cut through the trees. But what was that? The horse sat down upon its haunches, and down the long steep incline went horse and load hidden in a cloud of snow. This was madness, and the old man's anger rose. But when the load reached the road the horse was unhurt, and Norby saw, to his great surprise, that the driver was Wangen.

Norby went up with his whip. Words failed him. Then Wangen, beginning to unload, said: "You're trying to tax me with a forgery, Norby, but how about your own affairs?" Norby raised his whip and would have struck him, but another load appeared at the top of the hill, and again the horse sat down upon its haunches and away it went. And that was the way they used Norby's horses, was it? He'd give them a lesson, he would! But when the driver came out down at the pile of logs, it was Wangen again! How the d——? And now he unloaded and said with a mocking smile: "You're trying to tax me with forgery, Norby, but—ha!—ha!—what about yourself?" Norby again raised his whip and would have struck him, but suddenly caught sight of another horse at the top of the hill. It was the young brood-mare, and it would injure its feet in the slide. But it was Wangen again, and his lips were parted with the same smile: "I say, Norby, have you a good conscience? It's true the witness is dead, but just you wait!" And then another load came, and another; the hill was one cloud of snow enveloping a string of loads, and there were more coming; and Wangen drove every load, always that cursed Wangen!

The old man cried out and sprang up from the sofa, rubbing his eyes. Thank goodness!

"I must get something to do," he said, and put on his things and went out. It was too late to look at the timber-felling that day. He sauntered along to the pig-stye: but the twelve fat, yellow animals that had hitherto been his pride now seemed to him to be utter failures. "Things are beginning to go wrong with me," he thought. "And now in addition I'm to have this! That's the thanks I get for my kindness!" He sighed, and was passing on; but a pig put its snout between the palings and wanted to be scratched. The old man stretched out his hand, but suddenly drew back a step, for this pig too was——

A shudder ran through him, and he hastened out, and from a kind of curiosity he also went through the cow-shed. The cows turned in their stalls and lowed gently one after another; and he gazed, half in curiosity, half in terror, at each head, and saw that the first, the second, the third—ugh, what did it mean! He turned quickly and fled. He was beginning to see that hated face in innocent animals too. He slammed the heavy cow-shed door after him, and the lowing of two or three cows at the same moment added to his feeling of uncanniness.

"You great idiot!" he said at last to himself when he was fairly out. "To go and imagine things like that!" He was going in the direction of the stables, but turned round suddenly. He did not dare.

He began to think that his men had not the respect for him that they formerly had, and he was therefore unusually hot-tempered with them.

When he was driving he thought that the horses did not go so willingly either—as if they had a suspicion too; and he used the whip more than ever before, and drove recklessly. It was at any rate no mistake that his good dog Hector began to look timidly at him, as if he too suspected something.

"Don't be uneasy!" he said to himself, "you've risen in the esteem of your fellow creatures at any rate." The fury of the country-side against Wangen only placed Norby in a better light. If one man took Wangen's part, it stirred up twenty to range themselves on Norby's side; and as the old man drove along in his single sledge, dressed in his fur coat, people bowed lower than before, and those who had hitherto never bowed did so now. And the old man would laugh silently to himself. "The beasts despise me for what I have done," he thought, "but men respect me. Such is life!"

"They surely can't be merely making fun of me?" he thought one day. "Suppose they're only showing me all this respect in mockery!" The idea was unbearable, and he felt he must make sure whether it were so or not.

One day the people at the parsonage were surprised to see Norby drive up to the door, and come tramping in in his great driving boots. He was very cheerful, and as he sat leaning forward and stroking his knees, he told them that next Saturday he and his wife had determined to roast a pig whole, as he had seen it done in England, and if any one cared to come they might get a bone to gnaw.

Both the pastor and his wife began to laugh, for Norby always gave an invitation in his own peculiar way. And the old man thought: "They can't have any suspicion of me when they laugh so naturally;" and when they both accepted his invitation he felt himself secure.

He also dropped in at the doctor's, and there things went just as smoothly. And he was at the bailiff's, the judge's and the sheriff's; and when he finally turned his face homewards he sat and chuckled.

It was, as usual, a capital dinner at Norby. The old man took a special pleasure in being able to put such silver and wine on his table as none of the other magnates could produce. Both the pork and the wine raised the spirits of the guests, and the old man's face shone, and grew redder and brighter the more he ate and drank and talked. No mention was made of the great matter itself; but as Norby sat at the head of the table, and drank with one after another down the rows, or with all together, he noted in each glance and smile the very feeling he wished to see, namely: "You're a jolly good fellow!"

When at last the company were scattered over the two large drawing-rooms with their coffee, the bailiff came and drew him a little aside; and while they stood with their cups at the level of their chests the bailiff told him in a whisper that the judge had received the guarantee document. The bailiff had seen it, and he must say that Norby's signature was well counterfeited. But Jörgen Haarstad's! That was too foolish! Haarstad did not write like a copy-book, it is true; but his writing was not so crooked and illegible as all that, *that* the bailiff could testify.

"You fool!" thought Norby, and drank liqueur with him. "As if men like Haarstad didn't write their name in a dozen different ways. You *are* a genius!" But aloud he said: "Have you spoken to Wangen?"

The bailiff laughed. "Indeed I have," he said. "He declares that the signing took place in the café at the Grand."

"That's not true," thought Norby; "it was at the Hotel Carl Johan."

The bailiff emptied his liqueur-glass and continued: "But it's awkward for him that his witness is dead, and that there's no one who saw you write your name. And it gives a bad impression, too, to hear that a number of people are now getting bills from his general store, which they have paid long ago. He's a shady character."

When the sound of the last sledge-bells passed from the yard a little over midnight, Norby began to walk about the empty rooms, rubbing his hands, for he knew now for certain that people esteemed him as the old Knut Norby.

"But in the Grand café? That's a downright lie. I've never in my life put my name to any paper there. What a confounded liar he is!"

The consciousness that at any rate a fraction of this matter was a lie, now felt like a relief. No one in the world could prove that he had ever signed anything at the Grand.

"But I shall win the whole thing. I can be quite easy about that." And then a little later: "But shall I win?"

He sank down at a table in the little room leading off one of the drawing-rooms, on which stood a bottle of liqueur. When Marit came to get him to go to bed she was very much astonished to find him intoxicated, and she could not get him to move. An hour later she went with a candle in her hand through the dark rooms where the tobacco-smoke still hung in light clouds. There was a light behind the curtains in the doorway. She peeped cautiously in, and saw that the old man had sunk back on to the sofa, and was asleep with his glass in his hand.

# CHAPTER VII

DOWN by the fjord lay a little one-storeyed house, half hidden by large trees within a garden. Here lived Fru Thora Skard, the widow of the inspector of forests. Upon the death of her husband she had withdrawn from the social life to which she was accustomed, and henceforth lived quietly behind her flowers in her pretty little rooms. On rare occasions she might be seen going out to some sick or poor person with a book and a basket. Although she was more than forty, she was still young in mind; it was she who had started the young people's club in the parish. Any young peasant girl who wished it, was certain of obtaining from her free instruction in sewing and weaving. She had a little boy called Gunnar. Being a sincere admirer of everything national, she had her little house, after her husband's death, renamed and registered as "Lidarende"; and from that time forward she liked to be called Thora of Lidarende.

When she heard the news about Wangen she thought: "Poor wife! Poor children!" She knew Fru Wangen very well, and she was so upset about this, that she could think of nothing else. Although she had only a small pension, and was trying moreover to put something by for Gunnar, her kind heart said over and over again: "I must go and help them. Three children, the parents destitute, and then this crime! It would be wrong of me not to go."

There were such different opinions about Wangen's guilt and innocence. Fru Thora was sufficiently well acquainted with her fellow creatures to know that most of them believed Wangen to be guilty because he had already gone down in the world. She wanted to form her own opinion about the matter, uninfluenced by others, and therefore meditated deeply upon the matter, reasoning from her knowledge of the two men. For one of them must be in the wrong.

It happened that Norby realised in himself and his belongings some of the ideals that Fru Thora of Lidarende cherished. She had always thought there was something particularly Norwegian about Norby. The broad, strongly-built farmer, living in his large house and ruling over his labourers, was like a direct descendant of the old kings. In the store-house at Norby she knew there lay a quantity of old harness, drinking-bowls, sledges, and carved household articles, and she had speculated as to how to get hold of them for a country museum. Without her noticing it, or being able to prevent it, the impression from these things entered into her valuation of Norby in this particular case. And Wangen? He was the son of that magistrate who was noted for his animosity towards the peasant, and yet was not too refined himself to misappropriate public money; and now, whenever Fru Thora thought of the son, it was as though the atmosphere of the father surrounded him. Norby and Wangen opposing one another? Could there be any doubt in such a case?

It was thus that Thora of Lidarende's opinion on this matter was formed, and when once it was there, she felt no doubt at all about the matter, omitting to inquire into the origin of the opinion.

She did not, however, grow to dislike or scorn Wangen on account of this crime. On the contrary she felt it was just now he was to be pitied, just now he needed help. "You must not shirk your duty," her kind heart said to her every day; and she had no peace until she had made up her mind to offer to take one of the children.

She wanted, moreover, to set the parish an example in not condemning too severely one who has given way to temptation; and on the day when she fought her way in a snow-storm along the fjord to call on Fru Wangen, she felt light-hearted, notwithstanding the cold and wind, in the thought that even this sad affair could afford her an opportunity of doing good.

When she reached the Wangens' house, she was told by the maid that her mistress had been confined; but as this was the fifth day, Fru Thora was allowed to go in to her.

Fru Thora could scarcely restrain her tears at sight of this unfortunate woman, who had thrown herself away upon such a man; and when she bent over the bed, and Fru Wangen threw her arms about her neck, they both sobbed aloud.

They talked together for a long time before Fru Thora broached the subject of her errand; but although she chose her words carefully, Fru Wangen seemed offended, and curtly declined her offer. And when Fru Thora went away she had an unhappy feeling of having done something utterly wrong.

When she was gone, Wangen went in to his wife, and when he had heard Fru Thora's errand, stood silent with a peculiar smile upon his face.

"Oh, indeed!" he said at last. "They're beginning to want to take our children from us too now, are they?"

"But Henry, don't you really think she meant it kindly?"

He laughed. "Yes, of course! Why they mean everything kindly."

A little while after he said: "I suppose they understand that as long as I have my family about me I have a kind of backbone. But," he continued, going up to the window, "that she too——"

He stood watching the energetic little woman struggling down the road against a wind that almost blew her away. He could really see now that her errand had been one of which she was ashamed.

But she had come to the house trying to coax his wife to give up the child when he was not there, and when the mother lay helpless in bed. He suddenly clenched his hands in fierce anger as he looked after her. How she struggled against the wind! How her shawl fluttered! A shiver ran down his back as it struck him that she resembled a bat, and he thought of witches.

"Henry!" came from the bed. And when he turned, his wife stretched out her arms towards him.

He bent down, and when he felt her arms about his neck, sank upon his knees. "Henry!" she said, stroking the back of his head; "Henry! You mustn't think that any of us will forsake you!"

He could not answer, but took her head between his hands and kissed her forehead.

"Poor Henry!" she said again. "I never thought people could be so unkind."

When at last he rose, he said in a kind of exalted indignation: "I'll pay them out for this!"

# CHAPTER VIII

MADS HERLUFSEN in the meantime sat for hours together looking across at Norby. In his eyes Norby Farm was a kind of fox's den away there under the fir-clad slope, upon which he must keep watch to see what Reynard was doing.

At the approach of crises in forest prices, and of political elections, it was always against Norby that Mads Herlufsen directed his moves. When he won he slapped his thigh and was in good spirits for more than a week. If Norby were successful he was as ashamed as if he had done something wrong himself. But although these two little kings thought of nothing but doing one another harm, at the same time they were good friends when they met. They warred upon one another chiefly because there was no other worthy opponent within a wide area.

Mads Herlufsen now sat pursing up his mouth, looking across at Norby and wondering. "What does he mean by this?" he thought; for he was always accustomed to think this when Norby did anything. "It certainly isn't that he wants to quarrel with Wangen, nor is it for the sake of the money. There must be something behind."

At last he discovered that Norby wanted to get Wangen punished in order to frustrate his composition, and thus force the brickfields under the hammer. It was the brickfields that Reynard wanted to get hold of this time.

For a little time Mads Herlufsen sat rubbing his nose in disappointment at not being able to think of a counter-move. He did not care in the least whether Wangen were guilty or not; his only care was for Norby.

"Do I want the brickfields? Bless me, no! But why should Norby have them?"

At last a thought struck him. One of his farm labourers, Sören Kvikne, had once been in the employment of the deceased witness, Jörgen Haarstad. Wangen had no witnesses now that Haarstad was dead. Suppose Sören Kvikne could be utilised!

He remembered what an honest man Sören Kvikne had always been, so he took out a bottle of brandy, and sent over to the men's quarters for him, for the men were in at dinner.

It was not a customary thing for the men to be called into the sitting-room of the farm; and when Sören Kvikne went in, he looked about cautiously to see where he should spit, and scarcely dared to seat himself upon the beautiful chair.

But Herlufsen gave him a long pipe to smoke, and placed him on the sofa opposite himself, and after filling his glass two or three times, said to him:

"Weren't you once in the employment of Haarstad, Sören?"

Sören Kvikne fingered his thin beard, and gazed in front of him with a melancholy stare. Oh yes! He was, he answered.

"You can't remember, I suppose, whether Haarstad ever mentioned anything about having signed his name as a witness for Wangen and Norby?"

Sören Kvikne shook his head. He could not remember it at all.

"Well, well," said Herlufsen, "you must think a little, Sören."

Sören thought a little—but no!—no!

"For it's possible that the whole thing may depend upon you," said Herlufsen.

The man looked askance at his master; but Herlufsen was perfectly serious, and when he went away, told him to remember that the whole matter now depended upon him.

When Sören Kvikne came back to the men's room, he stood in the middle of the floor and asked in a loud voice whether any of the others had ever been in the farm parlour and drunk a dram and smoked a long pipe with the master.

At this there was a roar of laughter, whereupon Sören grew angry, and let them know that the whole matter between Wangen and Norby now depended upon him.

"Upon you?" exclaimed several voices; and some, who were reclining on the benches, sat up and looked curiously at him.

"Yes, upon me," said Sören, nodding his head. But there was nothing more to be got out of him; he was not a man to let his tongue run away with him.

From that day he had no peace either day or night. Whenever he met his master, he was urged on with: "Haven't you considered that matter yet?" It was quite true he had been in Haarstad's service five years, and it was quite true that Haarstad and he had often talked together alone; but—but—. He scratched his ear a great many times a day. He talked to his wife about the matter, and his wife too said he must think a little. And Sören did think a little. He thought both day and night, since the whole matter now depended upon him.

It couldn't be that time Haarstad and he—no, no, it wasn't then. No, if it was any time, then—then it must have been when they were painting the cariole together. Haarstad was painting the shafts, and he was doing the wheels and the body. They were standing in the sun behind the barn. And this scene, in which they painted the cariole, fastened itself little by little in Sören's mind, until he gradually became certain that if there positively was a time when Haarstad confided the matter to him, it must have been then; and when he came to think of it, it certainly was on that occasion.

When he told Herlufsen one day that he had thought the matter over, he could not understand why his master became so exceedingly affable. Herlufsen told him he might take a holiday for the rest of the day. He might go down to Wangen and ask to be called as a witness.

# CHAPTER IX

THE inquiry was now approaching, and the nearer it came, the more uneasy did Norby become. He had found no way out of his difficulty yet, and he began to fear that he would not be able to find one. Whichever way he turned, he ran against his own assertions; and these assertions, which now lived in people's minds and travelled by post and railway, had grown into a power, greater than Norby himself; they were like a son grown beyond the control of his father; they dragged him on continually, they compelled him with threats to stand on their side in this matter.

He would not go to an inquiry, however, for then he would have to take his oath; and he was not so far gone yet as to go there and perjure himself.

"I'm beginning to feel my rheumatism again," he said to his wife, when he was restless at night.

It occurred to him that there was a suspicious stillness over the country-side, in spite of what he had done—a stillness as if some one were lying in wait. He himself had no desire to talk of anything but this one matter; for he thought of nothing else, and was only easy in his mind when others listened to what he said, and had no time, as it were, to think for themselves.

But each new falsehood always cost another as its proof, and that in its turn another. He had to keep a constant watch upon himself, lest his tongue should run away with him; he was afraid of perhaps letting something out in his sleep, and hardly dared sleep.

But day by day the inquiry drew nearer, and he involuntarily began to grope about for a means of pulling through after all, if in spite of everything it should come to an inquiry.

But what he now had to get ready to say at the bar would be falsehoods again; and at this Norby stopped like a horse that will not venture upon an unsafe bridge. He pushed backwards; he was afraid; he was not accustomed to it.

No one is so much in the humour for philosophising as he who is suffering in secret. As he cannot talk upon the subject he would most prefer, he chooses something similar. One day, when Norby heard of the sudden death of an acquaintance of his in another part of the parish, a cold shiver ran through him as an inward voice whispered: "You will be the next, Norby."

That evening, when he and his wife were in bed and the light was out, he yawned heavily, and said in a tired voice:

"Isn't it a strange thing that we human beings, who may die at any moment, should pass all our time in doing evil to others?"

Marit sighed and smoothed out the sheet over the counterpane.

"Yes," she said, "it is."

"And when we look into our own hearts, we see that even those who go wrong and commit crime need not be any worse than one of us."

After a brief pause Marit answered: "No, not if they repent; there is pardon for them too, then, I suppose."

It was very quiet during the pauses in their conversation. The winter night was dark and cold, and now and again the wind was heard whistling past the corner like a dying howl.

In this feeling of death and the dark night, Norby again saw the parish—his parish; but this time all the people were alike, they were all ready to die, all cold, pale, suffering beings, such as one ought to be good to.

"Do you know what I'm thinking about, Marit?"

"No," came the rather sleepy answer.

"Why, that if we do something downright bad it's not at all certain that the consequences will be obliterated if we die. It's very likely they go on living and doing harm to others for a long time."

"H'm!"

"But can you tell me then how such a man can have peace in his grave?"

Marit expressed her opinion that our intelligence was not sufficient for that, and turned over on the other side.

The old man lay long, however, seeing a long string of Wangen's descendants having to suffer for this. Could he then at the same time be saved and sit in heaven? He lay there looking and looking, until he grew hot with anxiety lest he should not get any sleep that night either. He began to be sure that he had some disease or other, perhaps heart-disease. And then, while he stood in the witness-box and held up his fingers, it would come. He would drop down.

"Oh God, be merciful to my soul!"

At last he sat up in bed and quietly struck a match. Heaven help us! It was past two already, and he had not slept yet.

When he once more tried to go to sleep, he began to see how difficult it is honestly and fairly to put right a wrong done.

He lay with closed eyes and saw it all.

"If I wanted to make it all straight again," he said to himself, "neither getting forgiveness from God nor taking my punishment in a prison would help, for my wicked accusation would still live somewhere. But if I could find out all the ways it had gone, and follow all the threads to the end, should I be finished then? No. I should have to give compensation for the evil consequences. One will have forgotten the falsehood, another will have laughed at it, but a third will remember it and make Wangen suffer for it. But suppose I could make up for this too? Would that be the end of it? No. There would still be need to pay for what he suffered all the time people believed him guilty. Can that be paid for? No! No!" And he involuntarily shook his head as he lay with closed eyes. How was he to get to sleep?

The next day he roused himself and went up to Gudbrandsdal where he owned large forests, and where his men were driving timber. He felt that he must get away—he must forget.

Up there he was not a rich man dressed in furs. He was in a frieze suit, and went on *ski* through the forest; and the exercise and the fresh air did him good. He saw immense piles of timber, and it was his; he stopped now and again to look out over endless stretches of tufted fir-trees, sprinkled with snow and gilded by the sun, and they were his.

"If Wangen had even been a worthy antagonist," he thought, as he leant upon his *ski*-staff and surveyed his wealth. "If it had been Herlufsen now." But this man was down in the world, and did not own so much as the spoon he ate with. "And it's that poor wretch you want to injure!" he said to himself. "And not even using honourable means; for you're attacking him in the rear—attacking a dead man in the rear!" He felt inclined to thrash himself.

When he got home he had caught cold and was a little feverish in the night. He himself thought it might be typhoid fever, and that he would die; and he was tortured by the thought of the evil action that would live after him.

At last one morning he felt he could bear it no longer, and determined to get rid of the whole thing—first go to his wife and tell her the truth, and then go to the bailiff and make things right with him. Now it was settled, thank goodness!

But just as he was getting out of bed, Marit called from the door that there was some one downstairs who had been waiting for him for ever so long.

"That's sure to be the bailiff," he said to himself, turning cold at the thought. But when he came down he found it was an old farm labourer, Lars Kleven, who wanted to speak to him.

"Come into the office!" said Norby.

He was vexed that it was only this old man who had frightened him and made him hasten his dressing.

"What do you want?" he asked, sitting down before his writing-table.

To his great astonishment the old man came close up to him and seated himself so that he could look Norby straight in the face.

"It's a hard task I have to-day," began the old man.

"Indeed?" said Norby impatiently.

"I've come to ask you, sir"—he stopped to cough—"whether you've laid this matter with Wangen before the Lord."

Norby stared. He leant back in his chair and stared still more; and wretched as he felt, he could not help bursting out laughing. He thought, as he had so often done, that it was his father who sat there listening to this. And to think that one of his small tenants, an old clod, whom he kept alive up on the hill out of kindness, that he should come here and want to interfere in a matter that concerned only himself and Providence! No, that was too much! And Norby laughed. It was like an avalanche falling, and he shouted and could not stop, until the floor shook under him. Finally he did not know whether to give this poor fellow a krone, or kick him out of the room.

"And what then?" he at last managed to ask, trying to be serious.

The old cottager placed his hands upon his stick which he held between his knees, and continued calmly:

"I want to rest quiet in my coffin; but I'd rather not go and witness against you, sir."

"What?" said Norby, involuntarily drawing nearer. "Has any one asked you to do so?"

"Yes," said the old cottager.

"Is Wangen allowing you tobacco on credit?"

"It's God Almighty who's asked me."

There was a pause. Then Norby cleared his throat, and asked:

"And what have you got to witness about, eh?"

"I went to town with you that time, sir."

"When?"

"The time you signed that paper," said the old man.

Norby grasped the arms of his chair and pressed his lips together, and the two men looked at one another. At last Norby cleared his throat again.

"You're in your second childhood," he said. "You'd better get home and go to bed." He rose and turned towards the window, but then seemed to recollect something fresh, and looked again at the cottager.

"And by-the-bye, if you appear at the inquiry I shall have you declared irresponsible. Now go!"

"Good-bye!" said the other gently as he moved towards the door. "I only wanted to lie quiet in my coffin," he said once more, and then went quietly out.

Norby remained standing at the window with his hands in his pockets. It had done him good to be able to laugh for once; but it was still better to be able to be angry with some one besides one's self.

They'd better just come and interfere in matters that concerned only himself and God Almighty! If they did, he was still man enough to show them the door. They'd better begin suspecting that he was not happy! If they did, he would be man enough to show them something else. It would not be that poor old fellow at any rate who would make him break down. There would be no confession to-day. Some way out of the difficulty could still be found.

While he was sitting at supper that evening, Marit said with a little laugh: "Do you know that the widow down at Lidarende has started helping Wangen?"

"No." But it was a piece of news that stung, and he thought of that active woman with the bright face that usually smiled at him; but suddenly her face seemed to become grave, to turn away from him towards Wangen.

It would be a nice thing indeed if they began to doubt Wangen's guilt in the parish. If they one and all continued to believe in it, so that Norby could be at peace with God Almighty, he might still make his confession. But he *would* have peace. They must not think they could take him by force.

Something healthy within him seemed to begin to growl and rise in opposition whenever any one irritated him. He could not get this woman, who was on her way to Wangen to help him, out of his head. The master of the parish school, who had defeated Norby in the school committee, was a friend of hers. The fool! Norby soon saw him accompanying her in order to join Wangen, and at night, when he lay in bed, he saw yet others leaving him to go over to the adversary.

"Just see if my enemies don't make this an opportunity of injuring me!" he thought, and the anger that this roused made him still stronger. What a relief it was to be able to turn his eyes away from himself, and instead occupy his thoughts with what was possibly taking place in the parish! He wouldn't wonder if his enemies utilised the opportunity.

One day he heard that his old enemy, Lawyer Basting, was going to defend Wangen, and that he was not only going to insist upon an acquittal, but claim enormous damages. Wangen, moreover, had found witnesses who would prove that for a long time Norby had done all he could to injure his business.

Norby began to laugh, and then sprang up and began to bustle about with his thumb hooked into the armhole of his waistcoat. After a time he stopped and drew a long breath as if of relief.

"No, really, Marit! The wolf's beginning to howl now. Basting! So that hedge-lawyer has at last got a case, has he? Ha, ha! And then these lies about my having——No, this is really too much, Marit!"

"Isn't that just what I said?" said Marit.

From that day forward the parish was always in Knut Norby's mind, that parish which he saw best when he closed his eyes. All that every one now did was to walk along roads and sit in rooms and gather together and take sides in this matter. He guessed more and more who were gathering against him. He would perhaps be left quite alone at last; and they would make use of this in order to do for him entirely. Mind and health grew stronger and stronger in Knut Norby. It was too bad of Christian people to go and witness falsely against him. He had never wanted to injure Wangen's business, never!

He was in bed one morning when Marit came and told him about Sören Kvikne, who had been in service with Haarstad. He sprang up, and began to look for his slippers, and said, laughing:

"By Jove, Marit, Mads Herlufsen has had his finger in that pie!"

This eased him of his last burden. It was not hard on Wangen any longer now, for he had so many powerful friends, and besides he was circulating falsehoods. It now became as it were a matter between Norby and Herlufsen. Norby had at last found a worthy opponent.

There came fresh rumours. Wangen had asserted that Norby had cheated him in a timber transaction; then that he had defrauded the widow whose trustee he was. In his righteous indignation, Wangen did not weigh his words very carefully, and they all came to Norby as poisonous, irritating stings, exciting the old man by their positive untruth, and helping him more and more to forget the original matter, and instead to look upon himself as attacked, persecuted, and compelled to defend himself.

But the indignation he now felt only produced a growing improvement in his health, and he began in real earnest to prepare for the inquiry with moves and counter-moves. It was no longer a question of who was in the right, but of who would lose. It was no longer a matter between him and God Almighty, but between him and his enemies. Every time he heard of new witnesses appearing upon his opponent's side, his anxiety lest he should fail increased; and this urged him on incessantly to think of ways of being even with these men. "We shall see if they succeed!" he said to himself with clenched teeth. He recollected now the evil that many of these witnesses had done to him in days gone by. They were like old wounds, that opened and added their pain to that of the fresh ones. He became more and more angry; he no longer thought, but only looked about for weapons with which to strike.

The strange thing was that Norby began to be at peace in his inmost soul. The wound in the innermost recesses of his heart was forgotten, and he thought only of those that grazed the skin; so he began to sleep better, regained his appetite, and was in good spirits. He had a good conscience such as a man may have who, being innocent on twenty charges, forgets that he is guilty on the twenty-first. When he thought of all the twenty, he, as it were, told God Almighty that they balanced.

There was no longer an impressive stillness round about him. There was a noise. He went on with his preparations, went to his lawyer in Christiania, always recollecting new false accusations and writing them down, letting himself be wounded by them in order to feel thoroughly how innocent he was. If there came moments when all was quiet about him, he went on expecting new false accusations. He wanted them. If none came, he made some up without noticing that he did so. "Of course they say now that I disown this signature out of avarice. I! Or because I am afraid of my wife. Knut Norby afraid of his wife!" It irritated him that people could say such things, and he made up new charges one after another, without noticing that they were made up. They were like glasses of spirits, which always kept him in a hazy condition, always buoyed him up, always made him forget what he most desired to forget, always gave him a feeling of innocence and of being in the right.

The inquiry was now close at hand, and the old man drove about the country-side and collected counter evidence. He was quite ready for the inquiry now.

# PART II

# CHAPTER I

IN a room in a Christiania boarding-house a young man was sitting with his elbows on the table and his head in his hands. In front of him lay a large open book, with certain passages underlined with red; but he was not reading. It was Einar Norby, Knut's only surviving son; and he was a student of philology, and was reading for his final examination.

The window was open to the warm March sun, but now he rose, and went to shut it, as the noise from the street disturbed his thoughts. He began to pace up and down the floor, now and then passing his hand across his forehead with a pained movement. "What shall I do about this?" he thought. "For things have taken a different aspect now."

He was a tall, slim, fair young man of about five-and-twenty. His not yet having taken his degree was not owing to laziness. He had first studied theology for a couple of years; but one day he had gone home and had appeared before his father in his office to say privately that he could not go on with it any longer, that his conscience would not let him be a priest.

His father sat gnawing the end of his pipe, and when he had listened to his son's explanation, said:

"Well, well, you're quite right, my boy, to give it up if you are so sure of what you're doing. It'll be worse for your mother; but I must try and talk to her." So Einar went abroad to travel for a year and look about him, and on his return he had taken up philology.

A week earlier he had heard in a letter from his mother of Wangen's forgery, and it had at once excited his greatest astonishment, for he remembered with perfect distinctness how one day three or four years ago his father had come up to him and said: "Wangen's got the better of me nicely to-day!" And then he had told him about the guarantee, but begged him not to tell any one, not even his mother. This had surprised him at the time, and perhaps it was for that very reason that he remembered it so distinctly.

"What shall I do?" he asked himself over and over again. It was possible there was some misunderstanding, but he nevertheless thought it best to write to his father about it.

He had had an answer to-day. The old man wrote that Einar was talking nonsense. He had never had anything to do with Wangen.

"Is it nonsense!" thought Einar as he paced his room. His father wrote quite confidently that it was all nonsense; but Einar took heaven to witness that it was not. The more he thought about it, the more certain he was that he remembered accurately.

"But what shall I do?" he said again; for he felt that he could not at once give in about it. "Suppose Wangen is innocent and I am the only person who can save him. Mother wrote too that Wangen had no witnesses. What shall I do?"

The inquiry was to take place in a few days, so he could not put off acting any longer.

"And father writes that he has never had anything to do with Wangen; so it cannot refer to some other matter than the one I remember. Is it possible that father is so forgetful, or——?"

Certain of his father's ways in business matters had often jarred upon Einar. But this? No!

"But suppose that Wangen is punished for what he is innocent of? Could I ever be happy again?"

He threw himself upon the sofa and covered his eyes with his hand. Supposing he went home and put things to his father? What a row there would be! And if his father had really embarked upon something wrong, he supposed it was too late now to turn back, at any rate from the old man's point of view.

"But what am I to do? Shall I not do anything at all?"

The thought of what it would involve, namely, his going before the court and giving evidence against his father, made him dizzy. But if he were to interfere at all in the matter, he must be prepared for all that it involved. On the one side stood his father, and on the other the impulse to do what was right; and he heard a mocking voice within him say: "There, now you can see how easy it is to rise above family considerations! What if it had been some one else and not your father?"

Einar Norby had often been guilty of judging harshly, especially in the case of public men. He belonged to the generation of young men who, through bitter disappointments, have conceived a deep suspicion both of the ideas and of the men who had once aroused the enthusiasm of their early youth.

While he lay upon the sofa with his hand over his eyes, the mocking voice within him went on: "Now you must show what one ought to do. Be sure you don't show any family considerations; don't be a party to any corruption, like public men! Do what is right! How you have been applauded in the Students' Club when you have spoken of public men who float about on vague sentiments, and whose conscience is kept entirely by relations and friends. You once said that their meaning well was no defence; for they made their judgment drunk with sentiments that did not concern them, and thought they were honest, like the drunkard who believes that he alone is sober. Take care! Don't be a coward! Be sure you do what is right! It cannot be such a dreadful thing to come forward and give evidence against your father when you are in the right!"

It seemed to take him by the throat. There appeared to be no choice between the two things, either to be a coward, or to go home and bring unhappiness upon all those he loved.

At moments such as these, when a momentous decision has to be made, perhaps at great cost, there are always certain voices that lull and weaken. "You are a fool!" they said. "What in the world do you want to meddle with that matter for? Your father has one son living, and that son now wants to get his father sent to prison. Do you know anything about the matter? You talk a lot of twaddle about remembering this, that, and the other; but what about your father? Do you suppose he doesn't remember what he did? Does he generally act like a scoundrel? In any case, stick to your last! Leave to the courts of justice that which belongs to them, and see if you really can manage to be ready for your examination!"

This relieved him for a time, but when he rose and began to walk up and down, he once more saw the funny, white-bearded mask that somewhere in his inner consciousness began to grin. "Of course not, don't have anything to do with it! You might risk something this time, for this time it affects yourself, your own people. But talk in a loud voice when it's about persons that you don't know! Declaim then, and bring tears into people's eyes; but now? Be silent! Sneak off! Hide yourself! And start again to-morrow, when you take aim at some poor person who doesn't belong to you! Be one of those champions of truth for whom you have always shown such contempt!"

He grew more and more agitated. He sat down and passed his hand again and again across his brow, then started up once more and paced the floor, with his head in a whirl. He had scarcely slept all night owing to the same thoughts.

"I must come to a decision! There are only two days left! And if I sneak out of it now, it will not exactly be a heroic deed, and ever after I shall have to keep quiet when anything is said about justice and truth."

He looked at his watch. There was a train in a couple of hours. But just as he was about to get out his bag and pack it, he was once more seized with uncertainty. Suppose his father would not be persuaded? "What should I do then! I ought to have some plan of what I am going to do, if I *am* going to interfere."

He seemed to see his father, and Norby Farm in the summer, waving cornfields, and the calm waters of Lake Mjösen. Go and give evidence? Break with them all? Bring unhappiness upon them? Never more have a home at Norby? He sank upon a chair and sighed heavily. "No, I can't do it!"

# CHAPTER II

THE parsonage was not far from Norby Farm. The day before the inquiry Pastor Borring began to wonder whether he could not bring about some reasonable agreement in this wicked and foolish case between two honest men.

No one knew that Pastor Borring had a secret trouble that caused him continual suffering. He believed neither in the atonement nor in the utility of the sacraments; and yet as pastor he had to say and do what was pure and true. He felt that he was too old to resign his living and start again in life; and with his present good stipend, he could help on his numerous children in the world.

But this faithlessness to his convictions had made a very good man of Pastor Borring. He knew himself sufficiently well to judge others leniently. He took no interest in gossip, for he thought that the evil that could be said about others was not nearly so bad as that which could be said about himself. Many came to him with their troubles, and it was easy for him to comfort them, because their misfortunes seemed to him small in comparison with his own. People thought him a good pastor and a noble man; and perhaps he was both of these, because he was always burning with a secret despair.

"I'm going a drive to-day," he said to his wife.

"Is any one ill?" she asked.

"Yes."

"Where?"

"Out at the brickfields," said the pastor.

Enveloped in his grey ulster, with a red scarf round his waist, he seated himself in the sledge, and the little bay fjord horse set off in its usual trot.

It was a sad sight that met him out at the red factory buildings, where there was no smoke ascending from the chimneys, and the shop stood with locked doors and shuttered windows. "Poor man!" thought the pastor. "If he is guilty, all this trouble is too great for him to bear; and if he is innocent, this will be the worst evidence against him. He must be encouraged."

Wangen still lived in his pretty house, and after taking off his coat in the cheerful hall, the pastor went into the drawing-room. A servant was occupied in dusting, and she went at once to tell Wangen.

Tick! tick! went a little clock in its polished case on the wall. There was a sound of children crying in the adjoining room, and Wangen's voice hushing them.

The door opened and Wangen entered. He had grown very thin, his eyes wore an expression of suffering, and he was almost unrecognisable.

"Our little baby died last night," he said, when he had seated himself. "It was undoubtedly because of his mother's milk. She has had too much to bear lately."

"He means by that that Norby is to blame for this too," thought the pastor. "It is high time I talked to him. Dear Wangen," he said aloud, "will you do an old pastor a favour? Will you get up on my sledge, and drive over with me to Norby?"

Wangen started up involuntarily, and put his hand to his head. "To Norby?" he said in astonishment.

"Yes. We'll try and put an end to this matter, dear Wangen."

Wangen smiled and his eyes began to glow. "He's afraid at last, is he?" he said. "And so he sends you."

The pastor shook his head. "I've come on my own account, my friend," he said. "Let me tell you that it is easiest for the innocent one to forgive. Show this now. Come with me to Norby, and there I'll say: 'Knut, I want to talk to you a little, and Wangen is going to hear what I say.' Then we three'll go into a room by ourselves, and I shall say: 'You two, who want to send one another to prison, you're both guilty. Shake hands! Sign a declaration that henceforward neither of you will ever mention the matter again'; and when we go into the other room, I shall say to the others: 'There won't be any inquiry; for Wangen and Norby think that this has nothing to do with either the authorities or any one else; they have arranged the matter between themselves.' In a couple of days, people will have found something else to talk about, and in a month's time the whole thing will be forgotten. Now put on your things, Wangen, and come with me!"

But instead of this, Wangen sat down, and smiled a little uncertainly.

"And who is to pay the two thousand krones that Norby is responsible for?" he asked.

The pastor was a little perplexed. He had not thought of that, and involuntarily he stroked his nose with his thumb and forefinger.

"We-ell—But dear me! Peace between people is worth more than two thousand, especially when it's a case of going to prison. I'll say to Norby— let me see—I'll say: 'If you haven't given security for Wangen before, then do it now! Pay this! You'll never miss it!' I'm sure my friend Norby will be reasonable."

But Wangen started up again.

"No," he cried, "not for the world! Shall I beg him for the help that he's given once, but backed out of? Good heavens, no! No! Do you really think, Pastor Borring, that when first Norby has ruined me, then dishonoured me, then driven my wife to the verge of madness, I am going to Norby to ask him to be friends? No! That would be a little too much!"

"I don't know who is guilty," said the pastor sadly. "Let the guilty one settle the matter with God."

Wangen laughed scornfully. "That sounds very nice, Hr. Borring, but what have we got law and justice for? You should feel what it is like to be in my place. I spent my wife's and my own fortune in creating an industry here, and it succeeded as long as it wasn't in Norby's way. He has traduced me until I was refused credit; he has managed to prevent my compounding; and it is not even enough for him to know that I am destitute! No, I'm not to keep my good name either; I'm to go to prison too. And you want me to forget all this? If Norby were to come here himself and ask me—but it's too late for that too now."

The pastor sat for a while with his lips compressed.

"Tell me, Wangen! Have you never caused suffering to any one else in this world?" he said.

The question startled Wangen, and he again forced a laugh.

"All I know is," he said after a short pause, "that I'm innocent in this instance. And Norby has now tortured and worried me so long that he shall go to the prison that he intended for me. If he is so rich too he shall be made to pay. I won't take a small compensation."

"Ah! it's all very well suffering when you get paid for it," thought the pastor. "That man is the guilty one." Aloud he said: "God help us that we find it so difficult to forgive one another! And yet we expect Him to be always ready to forgive us."

"Do you think we shouldn't have courts of law to help us to obtain justice, Hr. Borring?"

"Judicial proceedings of that kind, dear Wangen, are a bad means of bringing right to light. They may perhaps get hold of the fruit but never of the root. Just you notice when the witnesses stand forward. They lie without knowing it; they raise a dust, and the court passes judgment from the dust. It is human; but God deliver us both from the sentence and its consequences!"

All this time Wangen was in the belief that the pastor had been sent by Norby, and that he wanted to entice him with fair words. He had therefore become impatient and wished to put an end to the interview. He rose with an impetuous movement, and began to pace the floor.

"The only thing I'm afraid of," he said demonstratively—for he was quite willing that Norby should hear this—"is that he'll get off too easily. After thinking it over, I don't think he ought to come out of prison any more."

The pastor felt as if he had received a blow, and rose quickly. "If he is in the right," he thought, "then Heaven help the right that has fallen into such hands! Can being in the right make a man so coarse and bad? No! He is guilty!"

He sighed and took his leave despondently. Wangen went to the door with him, and on the steps remarked:

"This is much more than a question between Norby and me. It most concerns the working men, who are left without bread. It is a social question."

"Indeed?" said the pastor, seating himself in his sledge, and gathering up the reins, thinking as he did so: "Of course! If a man only has toothache nowadays, he tries to make it into a social question. People are too cowardly to bear anything alone."

"Yes," continued Wangen, "I don't stand so much alone now, thank goodness, as Norby thinks."

"Then he's not so much to be pitied after all," thought the pastor, adding aloud: "Yes, I hear you've started a new working-men's union, and that you've often given lectures there lately."

"Yes," answered Wangen; "a man must be blind if he doesn't see that Norby has a number of rich men behind him, and that the end and aim of this matter is to do away with the eight-hours' working day in this part of the country."

The pastor smiled and said good-bye, and cracked his whip over the bay.

"That was a very unsuccessful visit," thought the pastor, and sighed. "People are only amenable to reason when they are dying; and even then it is in order to gain something."

Wangen had returned to the drawing-room, and stood at the window watching the pastor as he drove away. He could not at once regain his mental equilibrium, for, in spite of everything, the old man had left a good impression upon him, although at the same time this was something he was unwilling to acknowledge; for it might disturb the calculation respecting man's wickedness, to which Wangen daily added fresh amounts, thereby strengthening his righteous anger.

"How strange it is," he thought with some agitation, "that the priests always play into the hands of the rich!" The thought had half unconsciously been admitted, in order to get rid of the good impression. "And they try with texts and solemn faces to make the poor man give up his rights. I dare say!"

As he stood and followed the pastor's sledge with his eyes, he gradually let loose a whole series of such reflections, and little by little felt the irritation that made him believe in what he said; and little by little the old pastor driving along the road seemed to him to be a theological messenger in the service of wealth, like so many other priests in this world.

"Has there ever been an affair too rotten for some priest or other to lend himself, his God, and his church in defence of it? Look at war, for instance! And the doctrine of eternal punishment! A nice thing indeed!"

Wangen had nothing to do all day now, so he was always busy with this affair with Norby, and it grew and grew in his imagination. At the same time he constantly had to witness fresh sad consequences of his failure. If he only met the old tailor who had entrusted his small savings to him, he involuntarily went another way; for he thought the tailor stared at him with wild eyes.

From his early youth Henry Wangen had been intelligent and warmly interested in questions and ideas; but these ideas had always been aimed at what others should do, and how others should be helped. When finally an extraordinary responsibility had brought him to the last extremity, he was in despair at having to stand alone; he felt the duty of expiating and suffering to be a burden beyond the power of man to bear, and he involuntarily tried even now to turn the matter into a social question. He had at first, therefore, half unconsciously wished and hoped that this forgery matter was only the expression of a conspiracy against his business. Now he felt quite sure, and every time he could suspect some one fresh of being the rich men's accomplice, he became more comfortably certain.

When he really thought about it, he had long seen signs of something brewing among his connections outside as well as inside the district. Rich men were rich men, whether they called themselves farmers or merchants. They were all afraid of him because of his eight-hours' working day. And they not only wanted to force him into bankruptcy in order to be able to say "That's how things go with such a short working day." No, they wanted revenge. They wanted to send him to prison. They wanted to dishonour him so greatly that he would henceforth be harmless. He understood it now. Like many others, he had fallen a victim to the demoniacal brutality that wealth and capital breed.

For this very reason the work-people began to be unspeakably dear to him. He no longer feared them in consequence of having deceived them; they had become his brothers and fellow sufferers; it was in fact for their sakes that he was now being persecuted.

In this way the recollection of his regrets and resolutions in the dark railway carriage became less and less frequent, and in their place rose anger against the social powers, whose the blame really was. Nor was the oppressive sense of duty to expiate and become better himself, any longer any concern of his; in this matter, too, he could leave himself out of consideration, and look at society.

He turned from the window, and began to pace the floor. "So he was willing to let himself be used too, was he?" he thought, and the more he thought about it, the more excited he became. "Fancy! that lazy priest, who perhaps lies in bed until ten o'clock in the morning, grudges the working men a little ease!"

He bit his lip. By Jove, the working men ought to hear this! It would be a good thing if they could hear it all over the country. Priests were priests all the world over. He would have it in the newspapers in some form or other.

And Norby? He might send out as many priests as ever he liked. He should go to prison anyhow. Wait till the day after to-morrow!

# CHAPTER III

EVERY evening lately, Ingeborg Norby had sat and read the Bible to the pensioners in the little house. The pensioners were four in number, the dairymaid and the two farm-servants, who were all between seventy and eighty years of age, and had been in service at the farm for more than half a century; and the blind tenant farmer, whom Norby had taken in, so that he should not go to the workhouse.

In the little room lay the bedridden dairymaid; and in the larger room sat the two white-haired farm-labourers and speculated on various matters. They smoked, moved from one chair to another, and talked together chiefly about their various illnesses. The blind man for the most part kept his bed.

From the large house nothing was seen of these four persons. Even Norby seldom went to see them; but he kept them supplied with clothes and tobacco, although they all had money in the bank.

This evening the birch-wood was crackling in the stove, and the lamp shed its light upon the long table; and Ingeborg sat at the door between the two rooms and read so that she could be heard on both sides.

When she had finished reading, she repeated the Lord's Prayer and sang a hymn, in which the two old men upon the bench tried to join. When this was over and she was about to go, one of the men said:

"How is the case going on?"

"There will be an inquiry the day after to-morrow," said Ingeborg.

"Ha, ha!" laughed the blind man from his bed, while he scratched himself.

"Hasn't that there Wangen confessed yet?" murmured one of the farm-labourers, shaking his head sympathetically.

"No!" sighed Ingeborg, adding: "May God turn his heart!"

"If he'd only been wise enough to confess at once his punishment would have been lighter," said the blind man, still scratching himself.

"He may have confessed to God," said Ingeborg. "But the Bible says that if any one wants to do God's will, he must go and be reconciled to his brother. I'm sure if Wangen had come and asked father to forgive him, father would have forgiven him."

"Yes, God bless him!" said the dairymaid from the little room.

Ingeborg said good-night and left the house.

The two old men upon the bench began to undress, with many sighs over their rheumatism and pains in their limbs. One of them, after taking off his trousers, sat down upon the edge of his bed and lighted his pipe before drawing off his stockings. The other was also in his drawers, and now crept cautiously in his clumsy slippers into the dairymaid's little room, and seated himself upon the edge of her bed.

"Have you got enough on you at night?" he asked, as he struck a match upon his nether garments, and lighted his short pipe with a trembling hand.

"Oh yes!" said the dairymaid in a sleepy voice.

These two had been engaged, and had broken it off, and been engaged again, over and over again for pretty well a lifetime. For a couple of years they were not on friendly terms, and were each engaged to some one else; but then they became reconciled and engaged again, until things again went wrong, and so on. Since they had become pensioners, however, they had made peace and were good friends.

"Because you're welcome to one of my sheepskins!" he said, looking at the bowl of his pipe and trying to make it draw.

"Did you ever hear such nonsense! And you would lie and shiver perhaps?" she said. "No; if I'm cold, I've only got to speak to the mistress."

"Very well," said the old man, rising and tucking her carefully up. He came in every evening before he went to bed to ask her if she wanted anything. It was a kind of good-night. Of late he had induced her to smoke, for then he could always do her some little service, such as to clean her pipe and cut up the tobacco for her. But now, without saying good-night, he slouched away and went to bed.

"You've forgotten to put out the lamp," said the blind man. He could not see it, but felt its light upon him.

After the lamp was put out, the three old men lay and yawned audibly for some time, until there came from the little room a yawn so loud that the three men could hear it. This was their good-night to one another.

"It's coming on to blow and there'll be a storm to-night," said the blind man, drawing the skin coverlet over him.

"Then they'll have to have the snow-plough out again to-morrow," said one of the others, after a short pause. Then they yawned a little more, and silence fell upon the little house.

# CHAPTER IV

THE day before the inquiry, Norby was in his office all day, arranging his papers, making notes, and preparing his answers to the questions he would probably be asked the next day. He no longer felt that it was he who accused Wangen, but on the contrary he thought it was he who had to make the defence.

The grey light of a snowy day fell upon the table and his papers, and upon the old man as he stood with his spectacles far down upon his nose, and passed his defences in review. He was tired of going about collecting counter-evidence and taking declarations; but now he was well armed, and was only impatient to begin.

A slight smile came over the old man's face as he looked at a paper that he held carefully as if it were something precious. It was precious too. It was a declaration from Jörgen Haarstad's bed-ridden widow; and it would completely confound the evidence that Sören Kvikne was going to give. This was amusing, because Herlufsen would be disappointed. The old man was looking forward with intense pleasure to the moment when he should read the declaration aloud in court, perhaps with Herlufsen sitting there and listening to it. There was no doubt that poor Sören had simply been bribed to give evidence as to his having heard this remark of Jörgen Haarstad's. That was the kind of means these people used; it was really beyond a joke.

The old man began to pace the floor, sighing now and again. He was pale; of late he had been unable to think of anything but of how he could be even with his enemies. He had as it were passed by the actual heart of the matter in a railway train; and it now lay so far behind in mist, that there were far more important things to be thought of. It was clear, too, that it was not justice that his enemies were so anxious for. No; what they were striving to do was to injure him and knock him down.

At one time that scene at the hotel had stood very distinctly before him; but Wangen's assertion that it took place in the Grand Café had taken the sting out of the recollection. "Oh," thought Norby. "So it was at the Grand? Very well! Perhaps he's right. But then it's all the more certain that it's a lie. I've never in my life signed any document at the Grand. If any paper was signed there with my name, then it's a forgery!" Although these thoughts did not always bring satisfaction, it was nevertheless a relief to let them out. And there was so much besides to indicate that Wangen's hands were not clean; there were thousands of other things to think about and be incensed over, and the old man had now so often expressed himself regarding the affair, that to remember his assertions was the same as remembering the reality.

He was still standing rummaging among his papers, when the door opened and Marit entered.

"Didn't I hear you talking at the telephone?" asked the old man, looking over his spectacles.

"Einar's coming home to-day," she said. "He has asked to be met at the station with a sledge."

The old man put his hands behind his back and his legs astride, and looked at her over his spectacles.

"What do you say?" he exclaimed. "Einar coming home now? He must have plenty of time, that gentleman. He must be thinking of becoming a perpetual student!"

"You are so hot-tempered," said Marit. "You're generally glad to have the boy come home."

He did not answer, but again began to rummage among his papers. Was the boy going to interfere in earnest in this affair? He felt as if an enemy had suddenly stabbed him in the back. Einar? He'd better try, that's all.

"If only he doesn't first go and talk to his mother about it," thought the old man. "But that wouldn't be like him."

He hung about, however, on the watch to be the first to meet his son at the house.

When Einar alighted at the station, he found Ingeborg waiting with horse and sledge.

The mocking voice had at last forced Einar's courage up; and when he finally determined to go home, he felt as if he had burnt his ships behind him. He would put this matter right, and first of all he would try to bring his father to reason; but all the time he felt as if he were going up for an examination.

When he saw the old brown horse, the familiar double sledge and fur rug, a warm feeling seemed to come to him from home; and as he sat beside his sister, driving homewards amid the jingle of the sledge-bells, he was imperceptibly filled with the childlike happiness of going home. But these were the feelings that Einar had had to overcome before he came to his determination; and he was therefore on guard against them, for on this occasion they were a danger.

Ingeborg had met him at Christmas with the same horse, and this brought a host of bright, pleasant recollections into his mind. He thought of the ball they had given, remembered the doctor's daughter, who looked so pretty that evening, saw her eyes. His father and mother had done everything to make them enjoy themselves. And now? Now he had a feeling that he was coming home as a traitor in disguise.

"Why have you come so suddenly?" asked Ingeborg.

"To be here at the inquiry," he answered. "I want to see how it will turn out."

"Oh, you can be quite sure that father's all right," she said with warm conviction. Einar found himself wishing it might be so, and had to say hastily to himself: "Take care that your good feelings don't weaken your purpose."

"Poor father," said Ingeborg. "You can't think what stories people are telling about him now. That Wangen must be a dreadful man!"

Her eyes shone with confidence in her father, and Einar felt the infection.

"How are they all at home?" he asked, in order to change the subject.

"Little Knut has not been very well," answered Ingeborg, "but he is better now." At these words, Einar seemed to see the little fatherless boy looking at him and asking: "Are you really going to be unkind to grandfather?"

A little later Ingeborg told him that a young horse had been found dead in its stable the morning before. Einar felt for his father's loss, and seemed to be standing at his side and looking at the stable where the horses were stamping. And he thought how the beautiful creatures would turn their heads in their stalls and whinny their recognition of him, as if they too would say: "Are you really going to!" For he kept in mind all the time that he would have to go through it all.

As they turned up the avenue and approached the house, he asked himself again: "Am I really going to?" It began to seem dreadful.

When they turned into the yard, their father and mother stood upon the steps, as they always did when he came home.

"How do you do, father? How do you do, mother?" he cried; but the words sounded like treachery to-day.

"Come into my office; I want to tell you something," said his father, when Einar had taken off his coat in the passage.

"But you must come in soon and have something to eat," said his mother. "It's all ready."

When they entered the office, Norby turned round at the writing-table, and said, with his hands behind his back and his legs astride:

"I only want to tell you that your mother knows nothing about your letter."

Einar inclined his head, and the old man continued:

"And if that's what you've come home about, you'll have to keep to me."

"Very well, father."

"So that is what you've come for?"

"Yes, father," said Einar in a low voice.

The old man compressed his lips, but he moved towards the door, saying: "Well, let's first go in and have dinner." Einar followed in a shamefaced way, as if he were a naughty boy. He was old enough to see his father's faults, but he had a very great respect for him.

"Then mother knows nothing," he thought. "And if father is so afraid of its coming to her ears——" He dared not think it out.

The old man was quiet, almost cheerful, during dinner; but Einar noticed how pale he was. His mother seemed to have grown greyer lately, and he felt an involuntary desire to spare her; she had such complete faith in their cause.

He felt more and more drawn into the home atmosphere. He asked for news from the district, and had to tell his news from town. He had his old place at table, and was the son just returned home, to whom every one showed the most friendly face. Little Knut came creeping under the table several times, and up between his knees. Everything combined to draw him into something beautiful and soft, where he felt he must surrender; but all the time a good instinct seemed to be shaking him. "Take care!" it said, "take care! Don't let your good feelings play you a trick!"

"Now, little Knut," said the little boy's mother, "you mustn't worry uncle."

It sometimes happens that we suddenly receive a new impression of a person, as if he had in a moment changed his identity. Up to the present Einar had looked upon his father as the man who was unjustly accusing Wangen, and whom he was ready to oppose; but before he was aware of it, this same father was he who had been laid up last winter with typhoid fever, and was perhaps not quite recovered from it yet.

On the way home, Ingeborg had told him of all the false accusations that Wangen was spreading about their father; and now Einar too felt his anger rising, and at the same time a desire to take his father's part. As the atmosphere of home gradually brought out the feeling of being son of the house, he felt an increasing shame of his intention to betray his father, his own family. Here they were all sitting round him without a suspicion of the true object of his journey. He felt like a tyrant who was going to make use of his power of bringing, with a single word, misfortune upon them all.

After dinner he felt inclined to sit down and chat with his mother and little Knut; but his father, calling to him to come, went towards the door.

"God help me!" thought Einar. "Now it's coming." His purpose was already so weakened, that he heartily wished himself back in town. Little Knut wanted to go with him, but Einar loosened the clasp of his hands about his knees, saying: "I'll soon be back, Knut."

In the office the old man sat down in his customary place at the writing-table; and Einar could not help admiring the tranquillity with which his father slowly and deliberately filled his pipe.

"Won't you sit down?" said the old man, carefully lighting his long pipe, and then calmly lying down upon the leather sofa. Einar sat down a little way off.

"Are you in want of money?" asked the old man, raising his eyelids just far enough to be able to look at his son.

Einar felt slightly irritated at this question being put just now, and answered quickly: "No, thank you!"

The old man himself was a little embarrassed; for he had a secret respect for this son, who knew so much, and in a way was of a finer metal than himself. He would treat him as well as he possibly could.

"What was that nonsense you wrote in your last letter?" he said at last, once more raising his eyes.

Einar rose involuntarily. A voice within him seemed to say: "Be brave!" He began a little hesitatingly:

"I didn't mean any harm, father; and I still seem to remember that day you came up to my room and told me about the guarantee."

The old man laughed a little, and pressed down the tobacco in the bowl of his pipe with his fore-finger. "My dear boy," he said at last, putting on a merry look, "you've dreamt that."

"No, father," said Einar, in rather an injured tone: "I'm not a child. It's my firm conviction that you're mistaken in this matter. It's quite possible you've forgotten it. And I want to ask you to take back your accusation, for I suppose there's still time, and of course I know that you wouldn't do anything that was wrong."

"Are you taking leave of your senses, man?" exclaimed the old man, taking his pipe out of his mouth and looking at his son in astonishment, although he laughed again.

Einar bowed slightly, and said, "I mean no harm, father."

"Yes, you mean no harm," said the old man, trying again to laugh, "but do you quite know what it is that you're accusing me of?" And the astonishment with which he now looked at his son was more serious.

Einar put his hands behind his back, and leant against the wall. He had become more courageous, and all the time he heard the good voice saying: "Take care!"

"Can't you remember that day, father, when you came up to my room and——"

His father interrupted him with another laugh.

"No, Einar; you can't expect me to remember what you dream."

For a moment Einar felt perplexed. He had expected to be loaded with abuse; but this kindness and this cool assurance began to disarm him. He passed his hand across his forehead, and looked before him a little helplessly. Had he dreamt it? Was it really nonsense he was talking?

And though for his part the old man laughed, he thought to himself: "I wonder whether some one or other has been taking the boy in! It would be just like them!"

But now Einar raised his head.

"No, father," he said, "I'm not making a mistake; for you haven't put your name to any other papers for Wangen, have you?"

"Ha! ha! ha! No indeed, thank goodness!"

"Well, father, then you must take back your accusation, for Wangen is innocent!"

There was a pause.

"Take back my accusation?" The old man sat up, and passed his hand over the crown of his head, looking straight in front of him, and putting bits of his beard into his mouth. At length he said, with stony gaiety: "Oh no, Einar! It's you who are talking nonsense. So I propose that you go back to town again, and set to work upon things that you understand better than you do this matter." Saying which he rose, and took a step towards the table. Einar had noticed an alteration in his father's voice, which indicated storm.

"Well?" said the old man, turning round. "You stand there like a parson in the pulpit!"

"Once more, father, take back your accusation! Do, father!"

"You're quite sure your father's a scoundrel?"

"It's only that you don't remember, father!"

"Now seriously, Einar, what have you come home for?" His father looked actually curious, and Einar felt angry at not being taken seriously. So he said as forcibly as he could:

"I've come home, father, to prevent you doing something you will repent of."

"Don't you think, Einar," his voice sounded a little pained, "that I've got enough with half the parish down upon me? There are numbers of them only trying to get me locked up. And now you come too! Aren't you ashamed?"

Einar's head sank. "Father—but—." His knees began to give away under him; but unwittingly his father came to his aid?

"Who has persuaded you to do this, Einar?"

"Who?" Einar looked up suddenly, bit his lip and took a step forward. His voice trembled with anger as he said: "What do you mean by that, father?"

The old man could not help laughing at the lad's imperiousness. "I believe you mean to go to the inquiry and give evidence against your father!" he said, and laughed again.

"If you take back your accusation, father, I shan't have to." Would his father take him seriously now?

A deep flush overspread the old man's face. He attempted to laugh, to gnaw his beard, to pass his hand over the crown of his head, to sit down; but he did none of these things. He rushed at Einar, took him by the collar, and said laughing, but at the same time grinding his teeth: "Go! Go! And you shall go back to town this very day, or else—heaven help you!"

He drew back a couple of steps, as if afraid of being tempted to strike him. "Ha, ha! Indeed!" And he suddenly began to measure him from top to toe. He had only just become aware that the young man who stood there was no boy whom he could laugh at or thrash. It was his own son, who had suddenly grown up, and now stood up as his opponent—he too!

"*Will* you go?"

"Take back your accusation, father."

This was too much. The old man seized a chair, lifted it up and cried: "Be off with you! Go, do you hear? Will you leave the room at once? Be off, do you hear? Go, Einar!"

"Yes, I'm going!" said Einar, raising his head. He was so angry that he would have liked to take the chair away from his father and show him that he was too old now to let himself be struck. "But let me tell you," he continued, "that you'll have to leave off treating me in that way. Good-bye!" And so saying, he slowly left the room.

As evening fell, Norby drove out. After supper, Einar felt a longing to confide everything to his mother, but he did not dare. What should he do in the morning? Should he flee from the affair? It seemed doubly hard now that he had staked so much upon it. He went early to bed, for he was afraid of the influences that hovered about the rooms downstairs and the people there; they all seemed to tempt him to surrender.

In his little room, the birch-wood crackled in the stove, and diffused the familiar odour of which he was so fond. A metal candlestick shone in the light from the stove, and in it stood a candle of his mother's own moulding. He had fled from the good impressions in the downstairs rooms, and had run straight into the new ones here, that quite folded him in their embrace. The sheets on the bed, the clean curtains at the window, the recollections of all the nights he had spent here in his holidays—everything asked: "Are you really going to?"

"I shall never be able to do it," he thought, as he lay in his comfortable bed, wrapped up in his mother's sheets and blankets. It was very different from what he was accustomed to in the boarding-house in town. "But suppose sentence is passed on Wangen, and I might have saved him! God help me! I should never have another happy day."

During the night Ingeborg was awakened by Einar's coming into her room with a candle in his hand.

"What's the matter?" she asked, rubbing her eyes.

"Hush!" he said, for there was only a thin match-boarding between her room and the one in which her parents slept.

"There's something I must tell you, Ingeborg." And he seated himself upon the edge of her bed with the light in his hand. At first it dazzled her, but she soon grew accustomed to it. These two had always been one another's confidants, for Ingeborg was the nearest to her brother in age.

He spoke almost in a whisper, and she listened to him with wide-open, frightened eyes, and her breath coming quicker and quicker. She made excuses, she seized his hand convulsively, and said: "Don't say any more, Einar! You must be mad!" But she took his hand again. She wanted to hear all his reasons, and he told her them, because he needed to have some one on his side. At length she closed her eyes as if she did not dare to look up; she breathed still more heavily; something seemed to have given way within her.

When at last he left her, she lay still with her eyes closed. She began to be afraid because it was so dismally dark, and it was such a long time to morning.

She tossed about in her bed and could not sleep, owing to an indefinable terror. A criminal had found his way into the house, he was sleeping under the same roof; and this criminal was—he was her——No, no, it was not true! It could not be true!

"O God, help me! Help me!" she sobbed out in passionate ecstasy. "Help me! Give me a sign that it is not true!" But she suddenly noticed that it seemed as if God were gone. It was the first time this had happened since her conversion. What was it! Why did she not go on praying, instead of lying, her eyes gazing terror-stricken into the darkness. Was there no God? Had it all been a delusion? She had prayed that this affair might turn out well for her father. She had thanked God for his innocence, and felt a comfort in thanking Him. She had also prayed for Wangen; she had won this victory over herself and had felt a pleasure in it. And was it all a delusion? Had God made fun of her? Or did He not exist? Was that a delusion too? Was this comfort to her soul in being in fellowship with Him, this pleasure in doing good, also delusion, delusion, delusion?

She tossed about in her bed, weeping convulsively. If her father were guilty, then there was no God. It was all a delusion, a delusion!

"O God, give me a sign that Thou art! Give me peace! Is my father a bad man, who will give false evidence to-morrow? My father? O God, give me a sign! Help me if there be a God! For Christ's sake, give me a sign!"

At last she knelt in her bed, stretching out her clasped hands.

Towards morning Einar was greatly astonished to see Ingeborg come creeping into his room. She took his face between her hands, and said in a voice that trembled with joy:

"I must tell you at once. You've made a mistake, and thank God for it!" She involuntarily laid her hand upon her breast.

He lighted the candle and looked questioningly at her. Her eyes were positively shining with joy.

"Yes, Einar, God has given me a sign. You've made a mistake, and I was sure you had. And now you must go and ask father's pardon." She stroked his forehead with her hand, and disappeared noiselessly.

"Poor Ingeborg!" thought Einar. This young girl, whose hair sorrow had turned grey—this nun, who lived always with her thoughts on the other side of the grave—would it not crush her, too, if to-morrow he——?

"Remember, Einar, whatever you do, don't take any family considerations!"

# CHAPTER V

WHEN Norby drove off the next morning, his wife sat by his side. He always wanted her with him when anything serious was going on.

It was a grey winter's day, and the snow was falling fast. As they turned out of the yard, the old man's thought was: "I wonder how things will be when we drive in here again."

At last the day was come of which he had once stood in such fear, but which had gone on inexorably approaching. He was not afraid now; he was only impatient to begin, like the excited gambler, who only thinks of winning. A slight suspicion that some enemy or other had had something to do with Einar's behaviour the day before, only increased his inward excitement. They didn't know what shame was, those people! They bought witnesses like that Sören Kvikne. They tried to make the son rise against his father. But just let them wait!

The court-house lay near the sound, which is the centre of the parish, and near which the magistrates lived upon their farms. Along the narrow lines that ran across the stretches of snow and represented roads, people could be seen like black dots moving in the direction of the court-house. The body of the court would be full enough to-day.

The first person Norby saw when he got there was Herlufsen, in his great wolf-skin coat; and the first thing he did when he got out of the sledge was to go up and shake hands with him. Herlufsen also advanced to meet him, drawn like steel to magnet. The handshake was warm, and the two smiling faces shone with pleasure at meeting one another. Both were thinking: "I wouldn't be in your shoes to-day for something!" So Herlufsen invited Norby to take a cup of coffee with him at the hotel, but Norby protested that on this occasion he would stand treat.

The doors were almost too narrow to admit the big, fur-clad men. At the coffee-table they were soon warmly united in speaking evil of one and another whom they both hated. The great case they only ventured to mention very carefully, for fear that the one should see through the other.

Outside there was a bitter east wind blowing, which swept the smoke from the neighbouring factories through the driving snow. People walked about beating their hands together to warm them; and some went into the baker's shop and bought bread as an excuse to warm themselves. At length the magistrate arrived, the court was opened, and the people streamed in, stamping the snow from their boots as they went up the stairs.

When Marit Norby entered, she saw the pastor's wife and Fru Thora of Lidarende among the audience. They both gave her a friendly recognition, and made room for her between them.

When Wangen stood at the bar and protested his innocence, the pastor's wife turned towards Marit Norby with a sigh and a look, which said: "Poor man, how foolish he is!"

Thora of Lidarende already felt as if she must burst into tears. Wangen was so pale and emaciated; his throat was so thin inside his collar, and the back of his head seemed so big. His back was actually bent. Poor man! If only he would confess!

It never occurred to Fru Thora that her opinion of Wangen's guilt could be wrong, since she sat there and pitied him. From the very first this opinion had fostered a number of beautiful, charitable thoughts in her mind; and she therefore never considered how she had arrived at it. It was a view that had made her willing to make some sacrifice, for instance, to adopt one of Wangen's children; and a conviction for which one sacrifices something, not only becomes a certainty, but grows so dear that it actually acquires a moral value.

"Poor Wangen!" she thought. "Who can say whether all this is not really the outcome of an unfortunate inheritance from his father? But the human tribunal does not take that into consideration; it is merciless;" and at that thought she seemed to see before her a community with tribunals that were different.

Knut Norby was called as the first witness in the case. The moment had come for which he had previously felt such terror. He had to go in and say that he had not put his name to any paper for Wangen.

When he entered the corridor he felt the excitement of the card-player who has good cards in his hand, and is impatient to play them. His one thought was that he must not for the world forget anything. As his hand touched the handle of the door, a far-off voice seemed to say: "Turn back! There is still time!" But the voice was far too distant. "Did you really defraud that widow?" said another voice; and this filled him with a desire to knock Wangen down. As he entered the court, he raised his shoulders a little, as he was accustomed to do when he knew that a number of people were looking at him. The first thing he saw was Wangen in the dock; and when their eyes met in a flash, the old man felt a dull anger rising within him. He remembered all the reports that Wangen had spread about him. "You wait!" he thought.

On his way to the witness-box he saw both the pastor's wife and Fru Thora nodding to him, and it gave him encouragement. When he saw that it was not the magistrate himself, but his head clerk who was conducting the inquiry, he was offended. The magistrate might send his clerk to unimportant cases; but it was Knut Norby that this concerned. When the young man with the eye-glasses and the downy moustache adjured him to speak the truth, the old man felt a desire to laugh. Fancy that whipper-snapper acting magistrate! He had heard that this very gentleman had been as drunk as a lord at Lawyer Basting's last Saturday evening. And there sat Basting, too, that pauper, trying to look like a sage! He had come already to help Wangen, the fool! Yes, this was a court to inspire respect!

The questioning began. Norby found it easy to answer, just because Basting was on the watch. He had been on the watch, too, when he had tried to agitate for Norby's removal from the bank board, and to get appointed himself. The poor wretch's goods were distrained for the poor-rate, and he was thankful to get a bill for two krones to collect. And that man was on the watch against Knut Norby? Supposing it were he who had got hold of Einar!

"Wangen asserts that he distinctly remembers the place where the signing took place," said the clerk.

"Well, perhaps I might be allowed to know where it was, too," said Norby, innocently.

The clerk turned towards Wangen. "Wasn't it at the Grand Café?"

Wangen rose, and his eyes shone as brightly now when he said it took place at the Grand as when he said he was innocent.

To Norby this gave a welcome touch of comicality, and he answered with deep conviction: "That document was not signed by me."

At these words he heard a little sarcastic laugh from Wangen, which made him boil with rage. "I'll give him something to laugh at," he thought. "Wait a little!"

Then something happened, which came quite unexpectedly upon Norby. The clerk took out a paper and handed it to him. "Here is the document," he said, "and there is your name. Will you see whether it resembles your signature? You might possibly have forgotten the matter."

For a moment Norby saw his name, as he himself had written it. It had the effect of a ghost. He would not look at it. He looked at Lawyer Basting, who was looking askance at him, and this made him quite angry, and he threw the document upon the table, saying: "I don't need to look at that thing. I know what I've done."

At this Basting asked permission to put a question, and rising, came nearer to the witness-box. "Has Wangen never asked you to be surety for him?" he asked.

Norby looked contemptuously at the greasy-looking, bald-headed old man. He was about to laugh or give a scornful answer; but a voice whispered! "Take care not to let the cat out of the bag!" and he said with a smile:

"A great many people have asked me to be surety for them; but I can't remember them all." Then, irritated at again hearing Wangen's sarcastic laugh, he added casually: "He must have asked me, however; for latterly he was running about and asking every blessed soul he knew."

This time he heard Marit laugh.

When his examination was over, he remembered the declaration from Haarstad's widow, and asked to be recalled when Sören Kvikne had given evidence. When he came out of the room he stood on the stairs for a little while to cool himself before putting on his cap. There was a voice far away, crying: "You have lied!" But it was too far away, and powerful voices rose against it. It was true, was it, that he had defrauded that widow?

He still seemed to hear Wangen's laughter, and he thought once more: "Wait a little, and I'll give you something to laugh at!" He still had his best cards in his hand.

"It's too bad all the same," he thought, as he sauntered across the yard, "that one should be exposed to the attacks of such riff-raff. You have both to circumvent them and to wriggle away from them; but I'll be d——d if that man doesn't have to leave the parish now!"

Suddenly the old man stood still. A young man in overcoat and fur cap was coming towards him. Was he mistaken? No; it was Einar.

Norby was excited already; and now when Einar came, too, perhaps to interfere, he felt inclined to give the boy a thrashing.

They both stopped within a few steps of one another. Einar was very pale.

"Is that you?" said the old man, attempting to laugh. He knew that people could see them from the window.

"Yes, father!" said Einar, as he dug his stick into a snow-drift, "and it isn't very pleasant to be myself just now."

At this the old man laughed scornfully, and shrugged his shoulders. "No, of course not," he said. "Is a hundred and fifty krones a month too little? You have a family in Christiania, perhaps?"

Einar pressed his lips together, and his voice shook as he said, looking calmly at his father: "I wanted to follow the dictates of my conscience, and do what was right."

"Yes, of course!" said the old man, coming a step nearer, and laughing again. "Does any one forbid you to do so?"

"I shall have to go in and save the innocent man," said Einar, "no matter what it costs me." But he involuntarily retreated a step, and gazed at his father in fear. The old man still tried to smile, because people could see them from the windows; but he suddenly turned pale.

"Yes, I thought so," he said, breathing heavily; "but who has put you up to this?"

At this Einar flushed, and drew a step nearer. "Father!" he said, and his voice was indignant; "you must tell me what you mean by that."

The old man, however, resented the authoritative tone, and began to gesticulate, while he shouted: "Go in and give evidence then, confound you! Don't stand there and torture your father! Go at once, do you hear?"

He caught his breath and gesticulated with his arms, but no more words came; and he turned abruptly and tramped away, while Einar began mechanically to walk towards the court-house. Suddenly he heard his name called: "Einar!" He turned. "Yes, father?" His father was standing looking after him, but made a sudden movement with his hand. "Nothing!" he said, and went on. Pride had conquered.

Einar stood upon the steps of the court-house. There were a few steps to be made. "The fact is that father himself is the best proof that Wangen is innocent," he thought. "But can I? Am I cowardly or courageous? All I have to do is to tell the truth and save an innocent man. Is that so dreadful? Perhaps it's the only time in my life that a brave action will be required of me. I must be a man!" And he went on with slower steps into the passage, and knocked at the door.

# CHAPTER VI

WHEN Norby left Einar, he did not know where he went. He met some acquaintances, and had to stop and shake hands with them and chat, although he felt inclined to throw himself upon the ground and weep.

"There's no lack of snow this winter," he said, laughing almost convulsively at the group gathered about him, and at the same time thinking: "Now he is in there giving evidence."

Every one without exception spoke to him with the usual deference, and gave him sympathetic glances; and this gave him fresh courage. "He's welcome to give evidence," he thought. "But we shall see!"

At last he was alone, and stood at the window in a little general store. Above him on the hill stood the court-house, and he could see at the window the profile of a head with a hand raised to the chin. "Now they're enjoying the scandal," he thought. "They think they've caught me when they've caught my boy; but wait a bit."

It seemed to freeze something within him. This son, upon whom he had spent so many thousand krones, but who suddenly attacked his father in this way, was not Norby's son any longer. There was only a smart, as if something had been cut away, and it made him set his teeth hard.

"They are mistaken. If I'm not man enough to overthrow his assertions, I'm not what I thought I was; for now it's a matter of life and death in any case." He could not help laughing, but it was a cold, hard laugh; for the thought that he was going to disgrace himself and his son by having to refute his evidence in court, made him quite fierce. "As sure as I live, they shall regret that they took the boy from me."

When Einar entered the court, he saw at a glance that the witness-box was empty. The clerk was dictating something to be entered in the minutes. The witness's place was waiting for him who should tell the truth. It seemed to beckon to him.

When he shut the door behind him, the little noise made him start. The door was shut now between him and his father for ever. "I can never go home again," he thought; and at the same moment he caught sight of his mother among the audience. She smiled at him. She was flushed and perspiring with the heat. "If you only knew that I can never come home again!" thought Einar, as she made room for him beside her; and the fact that she sat there and made room for him, without suspecting why he had come, agitated him greatly. "When she hears my evidence," he thought, "she'll faint."

It must be done now, however, now or never. He felt that if he did not go straight at it, his courage would ebb, and he would collapse. It had cost him so much to make up his mind; to turn round now would be an insult to himself. He looked across once more at his mother, as if to say: "You cannot want me to tell anything but the truth. I tried to save father while there was time, but it was impossible."

He was about to address himself to the clerk, when Thora of Lidarende and the pastor's wife gave him a friendly nod, and he had to nod back again; and his mother beckoned to him, while the two other ladies helped to make room for him. Should he go there for a moment? He very much wanted to sit down. He had been wandering about for hours out in the cold, and the court was hot and badly ventilated, and he felt giddy and the blood rushed to his head. His mother beckoned again and smiled; and before he quite knew what he was about, he was sitting beside her. The two ladies with her gave his hand a warm pressure as they shook hands with him.

The next moment his mother was called as a witness. The clerk looked at her and said: "I thought you were sitting among the audience?"

"Yes, I was," said Fru Norby.

"But that is not allowed," said the clerk. "You must be good enough to remain outside when you are a witness."

Einar had a strange feeling on seeing his mother in the witness-box. It seemed to him that standing there she was in some danger or other; and when the clerk administered this rebuke, he felt an involuntary agitation. All his filial instincts were aroused and took up their stand beside her. He was no longer capable of thought; he only felt. After strenuously working himself up to a high pitch of clearness of judgment and truthful endeavour, he now suddenly lost his balance and fell into a strange world of indistinct but warm impulses. Far off a star beckoned to him; it was for him to go up and give evidence. But it seemed to go farther and farther away. There stood his mother, looking all at once so thin and helpless. The clerk had offended her. And was Einar now going up to contradict her before all these people? He might just as well go up and knock her down. He grew more and more afraid that something would happen to her out there. Nothing must happen to her!

When his mother had finished, she went out: and Einar had to follow her to see if anything was the matter, and in doing so forgot his overcoat, which he had taken off and placed beside him on the bench.

When he caught her up near the baker's, a sudden resolution came to him to leave her, for he could not bear this any longer. He was not equal to the task of concocting any explanation; he only said good-bye and hurried away.

Sharp hail-showers had taken the place of the snow-storm, and deluged him with rolling ice-pearls. The road meandered along the fjord and on to the station; there was an hour before the train went and he had plenty of time, but he hurried like a man who is running away.

At last he began to walk more slowly. There was a voice that whispered to him: "But this inquiry is only an investigation of the matter. It will be time enough if you give evidence before the jury." But he stood still, as if the thought were something that he could knock down. "Confound it!" he thought. "This is just as cowardly, *I* imagine I can go to the trial by jury? I? The coward!"

He had wandered backwards and forwards in this way before to-day, now determined to go away, now to go straight to the inquiry and give evidence; and when he finally approached the court-house with firm steps, he had felt glad and proud that what was truest and bravest in him had conquered.

And now? He could not go home any more. Even if his father could forgive him, he would despise this sorry hero; and as son at Norby Farm, he had betrayed the house and all his family just as much as if he had not been too cowardly to put his resolve into action.

He stopped and looked back. There, on the white snowy surface by the sound, stood the court-house, enveloped in driving showers. In Einar's eyes, that building was now only a den of injustice, in which false accusations were made and false evidence given, and where an innocent man was condemned, and had his life ruined. And he who could save him? He fled! He was the greatest coward of them all.

Einar suddenly felt it was quite impossible for him to go back to town and be the old Einar Norby. He could never look his friends in the face. He would have to live with shame in his heart, and always bow his head and keep silence when mention was made of honesty and truth in the world. Could he ever have another happy day if Wangen were condemned?

No, he could not walk any farther towards the station; his feet refused to carry him. At last he sat down upon a stone by the wayside. He had not yet noticed that he had forgotten his overcoat.

An hour later he was still sitting there, with his head in his hands. He was roused by the sound of sledge-bells. Two men drove past in a double sledge, laughing and talking about the inquiry. Something must have happened. But Einar sat on. Should he turn back? he thought; perhaps there was still time. And then he suddenly burst into a laugh. That this desire to do something great could still raise its head made him laugh scornfully and bitterly; and as he laughed he coughed.

When Sören Kvikne at last came into the witness-box, he put himself into an important attitude, and thrust his hands deep into his pockets; for he knew now that the whole thing depended upon him. He declared that while he worked at Haarstad's, Haarstad had once told him that he had seen Norby put his name to a paper for Wangen, and that he himself had signed as witness.

There was a great sensation in the court. This was an acquittal for Wangen.

"Are you sure of that?" asked the clerk, and looked at the farm-labourer.

"I remember it as if it had been yesterday," said Sören. "We were painting a cariole, what's more, when he told me."

The clerk now recollected that Norby wished to give evidence after this man, and as he scented something interesting, he determined to confront the two witnesses.

Norby had freshened up since Marit had told him of Einar's departure; and now his great moment had come at last.

When he stood in the witness-box with Sören Kvikne, he first looked round. Yes, Herlufsen was in court. He then took out his document, and asked the clerk if he might read it aloud.

"Certainly," said the clerk, a little uncertainly, involuntarily extending his hand for the paper.

Norby read: "I, Jörgen Haarstad's widow, hereby declare upon my honour that Sören Kvikne left our service six months before the date of the signature of Wangen's document. As he then went into service for some time in another parish, it is impossible that my husband can have spoken to him about this matter before he died."

The clerk now took the document and ran his eye over it. The audience had risen in their excitement, and the accused had also risen and had to lean against the wall for support.

"What have you to say to that?" asked the clerk, fixing his eyes upon Sören Kvikne. Norby had turned to look at Mads Herlufsen. "That's one for you!" he thought, thinking too that Herlufsen looked as if he had got the toothache.

"What have you to say to that?" repeated the clerk, as Sören Kvikne stood staring at his boots. "You said you were painting a cariole when he told you about it; but it appears that your memory is at fault. How do you explain this?"

But Sören was by no means equal to a new explanation, so he was allowed to go.

When Norby and Marit were sitting in the sledge in the twilight ready to drive home, a number of people crowded about them, and gave them quite an ovation. Norby had had his case in such first-rate order that all Wangen's witnesses had only provoked laughter.

As the old man took up the reins, Wangen chanced to pass. He looked broken down; and as he caught sight of his adversary, he suddenly came nearer and shook his fist at him. "You wait!" he cried, his features distorted with anger. "You scoundrel! You think you've won to-day, but wait a little! You shall go to prison, both you and the woman sitting beside you!" He made a sudden dash forward in the snow as if to attack them; but two men caught him by the collar and drew him away, although he resisted strenuously.

"Ah, that brandy!" said an old man, shaking his head after him. "I saw that there consul had him into the hotel and stood treat."

"The best thing would be for the bailiff to take him in charge at once," said another, looking sympathetically at Norby.

Norby laughed, cracked his whip and drove off, while they all took off their hats to him. He was tired. There had been so much excitement to-day. But he seemed to be sitting all the time reading aloud that declaration and seeing Herlufsen's face. He should never forget it as long as he lived.

As they turned into the yard at Norby, Ingeborg came out on to the steps, and said in a frightened voice: "Einar!"

"Einar?" said Marit, who was the first to get out of the sledge. "He's gone back to town, hasn't he?"

"They brought him here in a sledge," said Ingeborg. "I've telephoned for the doctor."

# CHAPTER VII

A BRIGHT moon shone out from among floating, silvery clouds, over snowy fields and forests in the dead of night. The buildings and the flagstaff at Norby cast shadows upon the sparkling snow. The sledges standing in the yard were turned up on their edge, so as not to freeze under their runners. A solitary dog was running round the house, giving short barks because no one let it in, although there was a light burning in one of the attic windows.

During the night, one of the old men in the pensioners' house got out of bed and crept to the window in his slippers. He stood there with the moon shining in his face, and looked across at the house. The other farm-labourer was also awake, and after yawning asked:

"I suppose there's a light in Einar's window, isn't there?"

"Yes," said the man at the window, hunching his shoulders because he felt cold. "I wonder," he continued, "whether there is any change."

The dairymaid could now be heard turning over in bed in her little room, and she murmured: "The dog has howled so dreadfully all night, and that doesn't mean anything good."

There was a pause. The old man at the window continued to stand there looking out into the silvery night and across at the lighted window in the big house.

"I heard owls last night," said the blind man suddenly from his bed, and yawned. "And I've not heard an owl here since old Norby died."

"Ah, well, Einar's always been a good lad," said the dairymaid. "God have mercy upon his soul!" There was another pause.

"It seems to me there's some one walking up and down in the big drawing-room," said the old man at the window. The next moment he hurried into bed as if he were frightened. After a little, the blind man said:

"Wasn't it in the big drawing-room that old Norby's ghost used to be seen?"

"If there's any one there to-night," said a voice from the little room, "we know very well what'll happen."

The moon drew two windows right across the floor. The big clock on the wall struck two, and the old men turned over and drew the coverlet over their heads.

The big drawing-room lay between Einar's room and that in which the servants slept. A figure was really walking up and down there in noiseless felt slippers. The moon sent a flood of light across the floor, and the frost-ferns upon the window-panes were flames of silver. But the man walking about there kept in the shade. At last he paused at the window, and looked out. It was very quiet out there in the night. The stars twinkled among the shining clouds, and lower down above the hills hung red and black banks of clouds, looking like some strange, variegated land. The old man wore his overcoat, and his hands were thrust deep into his pockets.

The door opened, and Ingeborg entered with a candle in her hand.

"How is he?" asked the old man, quietly.

"Won't you come in, father?"

"Is it Einar who wants me?"

"No, mother. He's spitting blood again."

But the old man shrugged his shoulders and answered:

"They often do that in inflammation of the lungs. Just you go back and take it quietly. He's so young and strong, he'll get over it all right."

Ingeborg went quietly out, and the old man began to pace the floor again. There was no use in fetching the doctor again; the complaint must take its course. But the old man felt he must be here because he could not sleep, and because the women wanted to have him at hand.

"Oh dear!" he thought. "I do hope Einar will pull through!" But the terrible thing was that sometimes he caught himself wishing that he would not pull through. Thoughts such as these buzzed about like stinging wasps on the surface of his mind. He was sometimes frightened, and sometimes would have liked to have given himself a thrashing; but the wasps came again. So low had he been dragged down in this confounded matter with Wangen.

Why of course he forgave the boy! He would never refer to the matter again, if the boy recovered. But—but—this illness had followed so close upon his anger; and it would take something to sweep away every little sting.

He paused again at the window, and looked out into the bright night. The wind was rising now towards morning, and began to raise snow-clouds away over the hills.

Oh, how pleasant life would be, when this nasty case was done with, and he could be the old Norby once more! Here he lived on his farm, and only wanted to be left in peace; but was he allowed to? No; they dragged him into this foolery with Wangen—wanted him to support such swindles as these brickfields; and when he wanted to get out of it, they threatened him with imprisonment. Then they suborned witnesses. And then they set the son up against his father. And why was Einar ill? If they hadn't persuaded him to come to this inquiry he would have been in town now reading his books, instead of going down there on a winter's day without his overcoat, and getting inflammation of the lungs. Supposing he died! It would be the fault of those who had persuaded him; and they would be sure to exult if Norby lost this son too, for they had succeeded in causing him to lose his eldest. His lips began to quiver as he stood in the moonlight. Would they succeed? Would they have that pleasure? And he turned suddenly, and walked towards the door. "I'll go for the doctor all the same," he thought; but then he remembered that the doctor had promised to come early in the morning, and he turned back to the window, and stood gazing out at the red and black banks of cloud in the north.

Supposing Einar died and went over there. There he would stand for ever, always looking at him as he had done down at the court-house, when he dug his stick into a snow-drift. "I want to follow my own conscience." Would he not hear those words night and day, and see that form, as long as ever he lived? Always this accusation from the dead. He might travel all over the world and collect evidence and declarations to disprove it, but it would be of no use.

The old man pressed his lips together again. No, the boy must be kept alive. Better that he should go to the trial and give evidence against him, than die and witness against him everlastingly.

The wind was rising. It howled round the corners of the house and in the roof, and up under the icicle-fringed eaves. In the east a grey band of light began to show above the hills, but the moon still spread her silvery veil over land and water.

Suddenly there was a sound of sledge-bells going down the avenue. It was the old man, in his fur coat with the collar turned up, hastening away to fetch the doctor. Einar must be kept alive. The poor dog, which had not been let in, uttered a joyful bark at sight of the driver, and bounded through the snow to join him.

It was still long before any one at the farm got up; only the pensioners in the old cottage began to yawn in their sleep. This they began to do an hour before they woke, and they always woke at four, from long habit. The dairymaid always had it in her mind that she had to get up to go to the cows as she did fifteen years ago; and the men dreamed of getting up and going to the forest as they had so often done in the early winter mornings long ago. The old habit had now become regular dreams. Perhaps when these old people lie in the churchyard they will dream the same things as morning approaches.

# PART III

# CHAPTER I

ON the morning after the inquiry, Fru Wangen rose at six, as she was now without a servant, and had to do the washing that day. She had scarcely dressed herself, however, before she was obliged to sit down. She felt so tired and worn out, for she had been wakened not only by the children, but also by Wangen several times in the night, and even when at last he fell asleep, he kept crying out in his sleep.

At length she rose to go down, but stood for a little while with the lamp in her hand, and let the light fall upon him. He lay curled up, his face buried in the pillow. Perhaps he was dreaming something horrible even now.

She stole quietly out, so as not to wake any of them. In the rooms downstairs the windows were thick with ice; and while she knelt and lighted the fires, she often had to stop to breathe upon her fingers.

At a little past eight she went upstairs to surprise him with a cup of coffee before he got up; but while she was on the stairs she heard him calling her, although he might have known he would wake the children.

"What are you thinking of?" she said, as she entered. "Do you want to have them wake up?"

He sat up in bed. "Do you know, Karen," he said, "there is no doubt that that Sören Kvikne, who came and offered to give evidence, was sent!"

"What do you mean?" she said, standing still with the tray in her hand.

"Can you tell me what interest that poor man could have in going and giving false evidence that was so easy to disprove?"

"No, no?" She still stood there, and hardly dared to offer him the coffee.

"No, Karen," he said; "the fact is that Norby had bought him. Herlufsen of Rud, who once pretended he was on my side, is in the ring too, as I might have known beforehand. And he lent this man of his in order to set this trap for me. Upon my word it was well calculated. It made me ridiculous, and increased people's suspicion. It was as diabolical as it could be!"

"Are you quite sure now, Henry?"

"Sure?" He became still more angry. "Sure? Good heavens!"

"Well, because I can't imagine how people can be so wicked."

"No, you can't imagine, although you have to see it every blessed day. I begin to think you'd rather it were I that was wicked."

"Will you have some coffee?" she asked, handing him the tray.

While he sat with the tray in front of him on the counterpane, Fru Wangen drew up the blinds to let in the wealth of snow-light from the bright winter's morning. Shortly after she turned to him saying: "I got such a fright this morning."

"You got a fright?" he said, as he gulped down his coffee.

"Yes. There was a man sitting on the steps when I opened the door; and I couldn't help being frightened, for it was the tailor."

"What?" he cried, putting down the cup.

"He must be mad. He's still sitting there. He said he would wait until you came down."

"Can't you get rid of the fellow?" he said angrily.

"No. He said he'd sit there now until you came. I'm at my wits' end!"

It was the old tailor, who had lost by the bankruptcy all his savings, upon which Wangen had promised him such good interest. He came almost every day and wanted to speak to Wangen; but the latter was afraid of him, because his eyes had latterly acquired such a wild expression.

It was not this tailor only who was constantly reminding him of the sad consequences of his failure. He received despairing letters, begging him for only a third of the money that had been entrusted to him; and letters that threatened and cursed him. People were continually coming to the house with tears and threats. It was enough to make one mad.

These people still believed that he and no other was to blame for the disaster. And that was not the worst; for in Wangen's inner consciousness, dark arms were extended, and he had to hasten to think of something else.

"Here!" he said, holding out the tray to her.

"But you haven't drunk your coffee!" she said in surprise.

He lay down again with his hands under his head.

"No," he said; "you take one's appetite away, Karen."

"I do?"

"Well, yes, to tell the truth. I can't think what pleasure you can have in telling me this about the tailor. I think you ought rather to ask him to go to

Norby." And he breathed hard, as if something exceedingly painful were working in him.

"Well, I'm sorry," she said, sighing; and taking the tray, she left the room.

Since the inquiry Wangen had lived as if in a fever. His tactics for asserting his innocence, namely, trying to prove that the forgery was only a link in a chain of conspiracies against his business, had turned out miserably. It had only increased people's suspicion of him. It did not, however, on that account occur to him that he had chosen a wrong method of procedure, but only worked his suspicion up to greater certainty. The belief in this conspiracy was just what had given him a good conscience in the midst of the troubles after his failure.

The trial, which was either to condemn or acquit him, was approaching inexorably. It was not the fear of being found guilty of forgery that made Wangen ill with anxiety as to the result, for of that he could acquit himself; but the dread he felt was of having his illusion concerning the conspiracy torn to pieces, and thus being obliged to condemn himself. Moreover, because this belief in the malice of his enemies made him feel good, it seemed like treachery in his wife when she defended them. He grew angry, and felt inclined to fly at her; she wanted to take away from him the plank with which he kept himself up.

He also had a feeling that it was only on the basis of this conspiracy that he had any right to make the working men his brothers in misfortune; so her slightest word in defence of Norby seemed an attempt to rob himself of a virtue, a strength, which the homage of the working men gave him.

When at last he came downstairs that morning the rooms felt very warm and comfortable. "Has the tailor gone?" he asked almost anxiously.

"Yes," she answered—she was standing in the kitchen, rinsing clothes—"I managed to get rid of him at last."

When he had finished breakfast, he sat down to the only work he did at that time, namely, writing articles for a labour-paper. The title to-day was "The Experiences of a Factory-Owner with Regard to the Eight-hours' Working-Day."

His recollections on this subject acquired a wonderful golden radiance from the very fact of his clinging to the belief that the cause of his ruin lay neither in himself nor in any thoughtless reform. It was an ideal that he felt an affection for, and he found a comfort in glorifying it, because it acquitted him while at the same time it cast a shadow upon his enemies.

As he sat with his pipe in his mouth, becoming warmer and warmer as he wrote, the kitchen door opened and Fru Wangen entered with her sleeves rolled up.

"Henry, dear," she said; "are you going to let another day go by without seeing about a house?"

"I've told you," he said, a little irritated at the interruption, "that it's no good looking for a house as long as I have this hanging over me." And he went on writing, when she continued:

"But would you rather be turned out? Have you forgotten that the auction is to be here next week?"

He threw his pencil across the table. Latterly she seemed always to be having a suspicion that he was doing something wrong, and must therefore come and interfere.

"Can't you go then and look for one, instead of coming everlastingly and interrupting me?" he said.

"I didn't know it was anything so important, Henry. And if you're writing something anonymous about Norby or others that you suspect, please don't go on with it! I'm sure you'll only lose by it."

"It seems as if you couldn't imagine my writing anything but what was mean. That's a nice thing to hear, Karen."

She stood a few moments looking at him, and then went quietly out into the kitchen, and went on rinsing children's clothes in a tub. She found it painful to live in these luxurious surroundings when none of it was theirs any longer, and when they never knew for certain at dinner whether there would be anything for supper or not. But to go into the parish—she—and beg for a roof over their heads, was the very last humiliation she would take upon herself; for this was just what so many people had prophesied when she married him. But why did he not go, when he always had plenty of time? Why could he not save her a little? These were the thoughts that had of late made Fru Wangen so bitter.

Wangen succeeded in recovering his happy mood, and had got on a long way with his article, when his wife came in once more and disturbed him. This time she had their two-year-old little girl with her.

"You must forgive me, Henry," she said, "but you haven't chopped the wood I asked you for; and now you must take care of the child while I go out and do it myself."

He raised his head and looked straight before him for a moment. Then he sighed deeply. She saw that he had something to say, and stood waiting with anxious eyes.

"Oh, dear!" he groaned.

"Do I bother you so dreadfully, Henry?"

"I thought you would help me a little just now, Karen; but I believe even if people came here and killed me, you would go out and in just as calmly, cook and wash, think of house-rent, and above all not forget to chop wood."

"It must be done, Henry. It's not my fault that I haven't a servant now."

At this he rose to his feet in great excitement.

"Are you beginning with that again? As sure as I live, I shall try to let you have back your money."

She drew back as if she had been struck in the face, and then she too grew angry.

"No, really!" she cried. "I won't bear that! I shall soon begin to wish that you were guilty, Henry; for to tell the truth, you become more and more unbearable because of this innocence."

"What do you say, Karen?" he exclaimed, turning pale and biting his lip.

"You heard well enough!" she said, taking the child in her arms and leaving the room. In a little while he heard the sound of wood-chopping in the wood-shed.

"It won't do her any harm to chop a few sticks of firewood," he thought; "for she takes everything else quietly enough, goodness knows! I wonder if they won't succeed in enticing her away from me some day."

While Fru Wangen chopped wood, she had to keep a watchful eye upon the child, to whom she had given some twigs to play with. It was such a shame that on account of this innocence, he no longer bestowed a thought upon either her or the children. It was as if she were not allowed to think about anything but his innocence, not allowed to feel anything but pity for him. It was not five weeks since they had laid a little baby in the grave; but he never mentioned it, and would hardly allow her to do so either. But it was his continual suspicion that began to weary her most of all. It made the whole world so exceedingly sad and ugly; and the worst of it was that she involuntarily began to be infected by it, like a disease for which she felt disgust, and which she would like to shake off.

And while he was resorting to more and more ignoble means for defending this innocence, she thought he grew a worse man. He oftener came home drunk than he had ever done before; he was churlish and brooked no contradiction. It was as if this innocence not only acquitted him of all the evil he had ever done, but it also gave him the right to do anything he liked, both now and in the future.

When at last Fru Wangen came in again, he was walking up and down the room.

"Karen," he said, "can you blame me for expecting that you will devote yourself a little at any rate to me just now?"

"But what is it you want me to do, Henry? I'm toiling from morning to night."

"Yes, you're toiling; but you might toil a little less. Couldn't you let my aunt have the children for a time? You know she would like to, and you could be sure——"

"Do you really want to send all three of them away, Henry?"

He stopped. "Would that be such a dreadful thing?"

"No, perhaps not for you," she said, and went into the kitchen again.

It was near the middle of April, and the spring had begun to appear. One day the sun was shining warm upon the bare fields when Fru Wangen stood on the verandah looking out. The river was rushing by, yellow and foaming, often hidden by alder bushes that were beginning to show green buds. To the right lay the shining lake, reflecting soft, bright clouds.

"Let me see, mamma!" cried the two little girls, as they hung on to her skirts, both trying to climb up and see.

At that moment she heard a well-known cough down by the garden gate. It was her father. It was always painful now when he came, and when he came on to the verandah breathing hard, she was sitting in the drawing-room with her sewing. He pretended not to see that she rose and held out her hand. The two little girls, who had run up to their grandfather, were also perplexed at his pushing them away as he made his way to a comfortable chair and sank into it. He was breathing hard, and placed his stick between his knees, resting his trembling hands upon the handle.

"Isn't he at home to-day either?" he asked at length.

"No, father."

"He used always to be at home before, ha, ha!"

The old man was over seventy, but was a very giant. His long white hair, thick, yellowish beard beneath his chin, and red, watery eyes, gave him a patriarchal appearance. He was dressed in black frieze, with silver buttons on his waistcoat, of which the lowest three were left unfastened to allow for his corpulence.

"How are you, father?"

"I? Grand! We're going to have an auction at home—sell every mortal thing; and your brother's going to America, and I shall have nothing to live on, and must choose between going with him or to the workhouse."

"Father!" she exclaimed in a whisper, her eyes fixed on him.

The old man laughed with his lips compressed and his blue-red hands trembling still more upon the handle of his stick. His head shook too upon his thin neck.

"Is he holding a meeting for the workpeople to-day again?" asked the old man with a bitter smile.

"No," she replied in a low voice.

"It's so strange to us old fogies, Karen, that the worse people are themselves, the more they feel called upon to make others better. Can you tell me what he has to say to those vagabonds—he, the man who has cheated them out of so much pay?"

She did not reply, but sighed.

"And those 'working men'—yes. They're amusing too. You may cheat them as much as you like, if only you provide them lectures to listen to. Never mind food and clothes, if only they can have bits of paper to go about with and wave. Yes, it is strange in these days."

"You don't think of going to America then, father?"

"No, not if he pays me back the last ten thousand krones; for he said he wanted them only for a fortnight." The old man laughed again.

"You can be quite sure he said it in good faith, father."

"Good faith! Yes, of course! And this good faith is now driving us out of house and home. That was good faith indeed!"

Fru Wangen again closed her lips and kept silence.

The old man passed his hand across his mouth.

"But I want something in return. You must leave him, Karen, both you and the children; for if I were to go to America, I should die in the middle of the Atlantic. Now I might perhaps get a living out of the farm all the same. But do you imagine that I'll live there and see strangers managing the farm, if none of my own family are with me? You must live with me; do you hear, Karen?" And he fixed his red eyes upon her.

Fru Wangen looked at him quite helplessly, but after a little shook her head; and as so often before, the old man went away in a rage, threatening that he would never set his foot there again. But in a little while she heard his voice in the garden, and going on to the verandah, she saw him standing at the garden gate looking back, with trembling hands on the handle of his stick.

"You've thought over your answer, Karen?" he cried. "For it's the last time I shall ask anything of you."

She could not answer, but made a helpless motion with her hands and went in, where she sank upon a sofa and began to sob. But leave Wangen? No, people would be right then!

When Wangen came home he told her that the workmen had determined on a demonstration on the first of May, and that he had a suspicion that they intended going to Norby Farm.

It seemed to her that this pleased him, and she rose suddenly, saying: "It isn't you, I suppose, Henry, that have thought of this, is it?"

"I? Oh, of course!" he replied, smiling a little scornfully.

"Yes, but you'll do what you can to prevent it?"

"Goodness me, how you do take on! To tell the truth, I'm not going to prevent it. To make known their opinion in a body is the only weapon these poor working men have; and I can't blame them for wishing to show Norby and the other money-bags what they think of them."

"That's just what I thought!" she sighed, and left the room.

It was doubly painful to her to despise him now when she was obliged to cling to him against all the world. It was just now that she needed to respect him; but the worst of it was that while others were trying to ruin him he was doing them the service of ruining himself.

One day they received notice from the liquidators that the works and villa had been sold privately, and that they must quit them at once. And so the day came when Fru Wangen had to go and look for rooms. There was an empty cottage on a farm close by that had been occupied by a schoolmaster; but the owner, Lars Kringen, had once proposed to her and been refused; and to go to him now——! But after going round to a number of houses, she came home quite discouraged, and remained sitting with her hat and jacket on. She had received the answer "No" everywhere. But a house they must have; and she felt she could not ask Wangen again. "Well," she thought, rising, "I may just as well throw the last overboard!" And she went to Lars Kringen.

A few days later a cart-load of furniture was driven from the door of the pretty villa. Upon it sat two children, and Fru Wangen carried the third in her arms. A little way behind, Wangen walked with bowed head, and hands buried in the pockets of his coat.

The little cottage stood upon a mound surrounded with fir trees, and had only two rooms and a kitchen; and when they entered, the difference between it and the home they had left brought them both to a standstill in the middle of the floor. The rooms were dark, the paint was worn off the doors and window-frames, the boards were splintered, and the timbers in the walls cracked.

Fru Wangen had to undertake a very thorough cleaning.

The greatest humiliation, however, had still to be gone through. They had to ask Lars Kringen for milk and provisions on credit; and on her way to and from his house Fru Wangen felt as if she could sink into the earth. But all this was Wangen's fault, and strive as she would she could not help a growing bitterness from rising up in her heart against him; and in all this poverty and discomfort, it soon came to be that they never talked to one another except to scold. And Wangen came home drunk more and more frequently.

# CHAPTER II

EINAR NORBY still kept his bed. He sat up among his pillows in the middle of the day, and each day a little longer than on the preceding one. As the days passed, he saw the last patch of snow melt away down in the yard, and heard the noise of wheels take the place of the sledge-bells' jingle, and the starling making a noise in the gutter over his head. One day, too, he heard the sheep being let out with a great deal of bleating in deep and high tones, and little Knut shouting at them from the steps.

To Einar this illness was a black darkness that separated him from something that had happened long ago, and about which he could not now think. As he emerged from this darkness, too, it struck him how comfortable he was lying there. He was a child once more, wrapped in the clothes his mother put upon him, and eating what she gave him with her own hand; he showed temper, and was exacting, and she scolded him; she washed him, and warmed his night-shirt for him at the stove, as in days gone by.

A recovery from such an illness is like being born into the world again. Worn out as one is, every little trouble brings the tears to one's eyes, just as they make the baby scream; and waiting for mother when she is away too long is unbearable torture.

As his strength returned, Einar noticed that his father never came to see him; and at the same time he understood that this was something he ought not to mention. It was also something that he ought not to think about; for there was so much besides that went with it, and that should not be allowed to come near him now.

One day Ingeborg came up with some hot water in a bath, saying she thought it was about time he had his feet washed; and as he put out his clammy feet, and enjoyed the wet sponge and her gentle touch, the tears came again to his eyes. "Oh, how good it is to be at home now!" he thought.

He remembered that during his first attacks of fever, he had felt horror at being tended by those whom he had betrayed; but that must have been part of the illness. During the feverish attacks, he had also seen Wangen standing in the room and saying: "I shall be sent to prison, and it is your fault." And Einar had screamed with terror; but that too had been part of his illness, and he had now recovered from it. Yes, it was a strange thing to be ill.

While his sister dried his feet with a warm bath-towel, he looked up at the ceiling, and thought: "Thank goodness that I was prevented from doing these people any harm!"

As the days passed, and he gradually became able once more to retain difficult thoughts, he felt a certain fear as to how it would be when he went downstairs and met his father. He supposed he would have to ask his forgiveness; but that, too, caused him a strange pain. Thoughts came to him. "I have abandoned a sacred purpose; and just because I am lying here and receiving all this affection, I am becoming more and more powerless to take it up again. I was to save an innocent man from punishment, and I was to stand a test of character. But I broke down. I took flight! And now I am lying and thanking God for it!"

"Mother!" he cried involuntarily; and if she were not in the room, he would be seized with an uncomfortable fear until she came back and he knew her to be near him.

"How pale and thin you are, mother! How often you must have sat up at night!"

"That's nothing, my dear boy. How are you now? Is there anything you've a fancy for?"

He felt these few affectionate words quite overwhelming, because they dispelled all fears, and for a time gave him perfect contentment and rest.

Ingeborg came up one day with some budding birch-twigs which she threw upon his bed. "There's a harbinger of spring," she said. "Now you must be quick and come out, and see what I'm doing in the garden."

When at last he was allowed to sit up, his seat was placed at the window. Girls were running bare-headed across the yard. They were laughing and joking. It made him smile too. He had had a lot of fun down there among the houses as a boy; there was a reminiscence connected with every corner, and these were now awakened, and all his ideas connected themselves more and more with the place and the people who lived in it.

Ingeborg came to him rather timidly one day, and asked him to let her read to him out of a devotional book, and he assented in order to give her a pleasure. Gradually as he listened, however, he began to think it was beautiful. He had been mistaken in this too.

One evening, when the reading was over, she said: "The lake is quite open now; the steamer ran to-day." And Einar saw the great open lake, its surface of a greenish colour from the melting of the snow. Logs were drifting about here and there, and a bird was sitting upon a solitary piece of ice, and floating along with it, now and again flapping its wings. He saw the steamer with its awning, and ladies on board in light dresses. Heigh-ho! Summer was coming!

"Do you know what father's doing?" asked Ingeborg with a smile.

"Father?" whispered Einar, turning his head towards the wall.

"Yes. He's having a little room put up for you at the *sæter*. The doctor wants you to be on the mountains this summer."

Einar turned his face to her and smiled suddenly like a naughty boy. Was his father really thinking about him and doing something for him too?

"Father hasn't come to see me," he said after a little, sadly.

Ingeborg sighed and gazed at the candle.

"He asks after you a hundred times a day," she said; "and when you were worst, he neither slept nor ate."

A little later she looked at Einar's pale face among the pillows; and though his eyes were closed, the tears were forcing their way from under their lids, and his lips were compressed. She rose, and wiped the tears away with her pocket-handkerchief, saying: "I think it's to spare you that father doesn't come. And besides, you can hardly expect him to come as long as he doesn't know what you think of him."

Einar's lips were more tightly compressed, as if something hurt him.

"Shall I ask father to come, Einar?"

"Yes," he whispered.

Norby had said to his wife that there had been a disagreement between himself and Einar, and that he would not go in to see him until the boy was well enough to talk about the matter.

He had gradually become quite sure that his enemies had incited the boy against him; but who could have been knowing enough for that? Einar! Yes, it was well done.

But how anxiously he had waited to see whether Einar would send to him; for after the manner in which they had parted, he did not feel able to see him until he yielded. But would he yield? Should he get his boy back?

What were his thoughts now when the moment came at last? He went slowly up the stairs, but had to hold tight to the banisters. When he entered the room, he saw at once how emaciated the boy was. The thin beard that had been allowed to grow while he was ill made him unrecognisable. Einar's eyes were still wet, and he smiled anxiously as he held out his hand.

Ingeborg had come up again with him, but slipped quietly out when she saw her father's emotion; and the two were left alone. The old man's lips were compressed as he seated himself and took his son's outstretched hand. It was so damp and nerveless and thin that he was quite afraid to take hold of it. Einar saw his father's emotion, and worn and excited as he was already, he burst into tears.

"Forgive me, father!"

The old man rose and arranged the coverlet better about his son.

"Don't talk about it!" he managed to say. "And you musn't take this to heart now; it's bad for you."

When, a little later, the old man once more stood alone in his office, he was sniffing as if he had a cold.

"Heaven be praised!" he said, with his eyes raised to the ceiling. "Thank God that I have got my boy back again!"

He sank upon the leather sofa, and sat staring in front of him, his lips trembling. Nothing so great had ever happened at Norby before. And so there was a higher purpose in this illness. He understood it now.

"Thank God!" he said again, with his eyes raised to the ceiling.

When a woman gets back her child that robbers have taken, one can understand that her joy is unbounded, but that her hatred of those who took him from her, her fear of their coming again, and her desire to render them harmless, are just as great as her happiness. It was the same with Norby now. In the midst of his joy he thought of Wangen. "They didn't succeed," he thought. "There's One who's stronger than all their artifices." While he sat and thanked God in an indescribable feeling of happiness, he saw Wangen and his other enemies as evil forces that might come again; but they should really be made harmless now. "He shall leave the district!" he thought, in mingled anger and pleasure. "He's done harm enough now. He shan't only go to jail; he ought to be transported!" And if Norby's best friend had now said to him: "But you have guaranteed for this same Wangen," Norby would have knocked him down. For God knows it was false. Could the hands be clean of a man who had recourse to such tricks? No, no, no! If a thought such as this crossed the old man's mind, it filled him with disgust, and he felt he must spit it out. No, he was completely in the right. That devil actually declared that Norby had signed his document at the Grand! Good gracious!

"I thank Thee, O God!—But he shall be turned out of the district!"

# CHAPTER III

THE day came at length on which Fru Wangen's father and brother were to leave their farm. She had determined to get up very early in order to go and help them with anything that might be wanted; but at four o'clock she was awakened by somebody knocking at their door. She was surprised, but got up, put something on, and went to the door, and asked who was there.

It was her brother. When she opened the door, she saw in the grey light that he looked quite distracted.

"Is anything the matter?" she asked.

"Father!" he whispered in a terrified whisper, and remained standing outside.

"Do come in! What's the matter with father?"

Her brother did not answer immediately, but walked past her into the room, and sat down heavily. By this time she was so frightened that she did not dare to ask, but stood dumbly waiting.

And as she stood there in the half-light, with her shawl wrapped round her, her brother told her, as carefully as he could, that the evening before they had missed his father, and had been round the neighbourhood, searching and inquiring. And at last they had found him hanging in the barn at home.

When Wangen at last came down in the morning he found his wife sitting in the same scanty attire in the sitting-room, staring straight before her. There was no coffee made, nothing was done; she only sat there.

"Why, Karen! What is it?"

"Nothing," she said huskily.

This day, too, she had to go about and see to the day's work. The eldest girl had to go to school, the two younger ones to be taken care of, and the usual errands to be gone up to the farm to fetch food and milk. But all the time her old father seemed to be with her. Rather than leave the home of his ancestors in poverty he had parted with life. She could see him hanging by his thin neck in the barn where she had so often played blind man's buff; and all the time he kept saying: "It is your fault! Why did you marry him? Now you see!"

Great exertion was needed to make her feet carry her where she had to go.

When Wangen heard it, he sat motionless for some time, his face buried in his hands. The image of this old man, whom he had driven to death by his recklessness, took him back once more to that afternoon in the dark railway carriage when self-knowledge and cold responsibility had overwhelmed him as a superhuman burden.

"Oh!" he cried suddenly, starting up, "this is too much, Karen! I can't bear it; you must help me!"

"I think you ought to help me," she replied monotonously, without looking at him.

Later in the day he came in and found her again sitting and gazing straight before her, motionless and far away, although their youngest child was standing crying and pulling at her skirts. And when she fixed her eyes upon him he started involuntarily. He did not know whether her gaze was full of terror of him, or whether it was hatred.

"Now she thinks this is my fault, and she'll say so soon!" he thought; and although he knew it was true, he felt a desire to oppose and keep her at a distance. "As if I hadn't enough to bear already!" he thought. "And she wants to throw this upon me!" And he worked himself up to still greater irritation against her, as if this new misfortune had been in some way or other due to her.

They went about in fear of one another, each keeping silence from a suspicion that the other was ready to recriminate. They had been torn from the home in which they had passed happy years, and the discomfort and poverty of the miserable cottage only helped to remind them of their misfortune and keep them apart.

While Fru Wangen was standing in the kitchen making some soup for the children, she suddenly sank into a chair and stared into the fire with terrified eyes, for her father, as he hung there, said that he did not mind about Wangen. It was only she he troubled about, she who had brought him into the family.

It was she! It was she!

The soup boiled over, and Fru Wangen did not notice it. The floor seemed to be sliding away from under her, and she thought that something black stretched out hands towards her until she turned cold with terror, and began involuntarily to look for something to save her.

It was the bankruptcy that had ruined them all. But supposing that Wangen were really innocent? Then her father might have made his speech to those who were guilty. She also now saw in Wangen's innocence a plank to which she could cling. He was innocent; he must be innocent.

Later in the day Wangen had gone to her father's farm, as she did not feel equal to it; but he turned back, too, when he saw the house. He dared not see the dead man.

When he came home, his wife was sitting alone with her elbows upon the table and her chin resting in her hands.

"Where are the children?" he asked at once, looking round.

"They're sent away," she said in a dull tone, looking at him.

An uncomfortable suspicion suddenly crossed his mind.

"But tell me where they are," he said, opening the door to the other room; but there was no one there.

"I telephoned for your aunt," she said in the same tone as before. "She came at once, and drove away a little while ago." And as he still stood and looked at her a little uncertainly, she added, "I thought it would be better for you, Henry. Is there anything you would like me to help you with?"

It sounded so mysterious. He did not thank her, because he felt it was not to him she spoke, but to herself.

It was uncomfortably empty in the bedroom when they went to bed that night. The children's places were empty.

Although Fru Wangen had been frightened into turning to her husband, clung to his innocence, and felt a desire to support him and show him confidence, she could not speak to him yet; for she did not want to say anything unkind, and she could not yet say anything kind. The silence was all the greater because there was no sound of whimpering, no gentle breathing, no little bodies turning over in bed or requiring covering. Husband and wife were thrown back upon each other, and the silence and the breach between them forced them to look into themselves, where each saw the old man hanging in the barn.

Wangen was in bed before his wife, and lay looking at her. It took her so long to undress; it was as though she dreaded going to bed. Now and again she looked round bewildered, as if she expected to find the children there after all.

"It's not my fault this time at any rate," he thought; "but she'll lay the blame on to me all the same."

When at last she was in bed, lying on her back with her hands under her head, looking up at the ceiling, he had an uncomfortable feeling that she was capable of anything, perhaps that very night when he was asleep. A tallow candle was burning on a stool by his bedside, but he dared not put it out.

"Aren't you going to put out the candle?" she asked in a dull voice, still looking up at the ceiling.

He had to put it out at last. The grey light of the spring night showed in the window, which had no blind, and they both lay with wide-open eyes fixed on this faint light, as if they were afraid of closing them or looking into darkness. Neither of them had any pretext for rising to attend to one or other of the children; so they were forced to lie still and let the thoughts put up their heads out of the night. She seemed to see her father as he was the last time he came to her, saw him down in the garden, heard his opinion of her husband. "Why wasn't I more compliant then?" she thought. "It's too late now! I can never make up for it! What have I done?"

Wangen lived over again the scene when he had borrowed the last ten thousand krones. He lied, he exaggerated, he persuaded—and believed in it. That was how it seemed with all his ideals now. He believed in them; they intoxicated him slightly; but just look at the consequences!

He involuntarily began to tremble in his bed, for he felt as if he would have to drag the dead body of the old man after him for ever and ever. Fru Wangen noticed his distress, and it made her own greater. "Is it his fault after all?" she thought, and felt her anger rise. But in that case it would be her fault too. No, he was innocent; he must be innocent. The desire to hold him up insensibly gained the upper hand, and she put out her hand towards him.

"Take hold of my hand, Henry!"

And when their hands lay in one another's—the two alone together—they were as they had been when they were newly married and fell asleep with fingers intertwined.

"Shouldn't I have married him when I was fond of him?" she thought, as if her father could hear; and she insensibly conjured up the memory of the beautiful moments in their early love, as if to convince herself that she was honest now.

But her father had objections to make—hanging there—and she involuntarily pressed her husband's hand closer. This union of their hands in affection gave their fear another direction. They were at last able to occupy themselves with others, and therefore began to be sorry for one another, because that kept them from seeing to the bottom of their own misery.

"My poor Karen!" said Wangen. "It's worst for you after all."

She loosed his hand to stroke his wrist, and answered in a low voice: "Oh no, Henry! It's worst for you. Good heavens!"

"No, Karen, for I'm a man; and he was your father."

The last words gave her a shock, and once more brought the image of the dead man before her eyes. But she could not stand this any longer. It couldn't be Wangen's fault. And insensibly she took refuge in Wangen, in his innocence, wherein now lay her only safety.

"Henry, may I come into your bed?"

"Yes, dear."

He too was glad not to feel alone any more. He held up the bedclothes, and she crept in, and as in the old days laid her head upon his shoulder, clung to him so as to feel safe and calm.

He covered her up carefully, and put his arms about her. The confidence of each inspired the other, and they took refuge in one another, in the hope of finding the good conscience they both sought for. And as the warmth of one body was imparted to the other, and they became one, they began involuntarily to talk of their common excuse, as if to convince themselves each through the other.

After lying a little while, she said softly, against his cheek, with a sigh: "Oh dear! All this wouldn't have happened, if——"

He understood what she meant, and passed his disengaged hand across his forehead. "No," he said, "it wouldn't." And at the words they both saw Norby and the rich men as the powers of evil against which their indignation might rise; and instead of feeling themselves guilty, they began to feel themselves as a kind of champions of right and truth. For him especially it was so good to hear this from her; for now she no longer doubted either.

Outside the spring night was passing slowly. They could hear the sound of rain on the doorstep, and of the brook that ran down past their house from the little valley.

She had been lying some time looking at the window, when she said: "Perhaps Haarstad's widow was pressed into making that declaration too!"

"Yes!" said he, stretching himself.

This suspicion of his, that she had abhorred before, she now felt a desire to cling to; there was a relief, a kind of acquittal in it.

They tried to close their eyes and be silent, but neither of them could sleep, and both wanted to go on listening to their defence.

"Well, now they'll go to America, most of the work-people," he said, and left her to say the rest. And in a little while she said: "All those who can work are likely to go, when things are managed as they are here."

He felt such pleasure and comfort every time she said what he had so often said. She was quite on his side at last. At last she, too, felt convinced.

"And you had thought of establishing a pension fund for them, too," she said.

"Yes, if I could only have gone on."

"And how well the working men lived! I remember when their wives brought them their meals how pleased and happy they looked!"

"Yes, it's different now," said he.

The night was very long; but they kept close to one another, and talked at intervals about the same thing, as if it were a fire that had to be kept up. She even ventured to say: "Don't you think people would have got pretty good interest on their money, if only you could have gone on in peace?"

"Yes, of course! Why, it was improving all the time—until the rich men grew frightened."

"Yes, I haven't understood until now, what a disappointment it must have been for you," she said with feeling; and burying her head in his shoulder she whispered: "Can you forgive me, Henry? I haven't been what I should have been."

He was touched. "Forgive?" he said. "Why, I've nothing to forgive! You've been so clever, Karen, and have had so much to see to. But I'll help you now."

"Don't talk like that, Henry! I see now that you must have felt paralysed."

Thus the night passed. They talked themselves more and more together, and found their own confidence in one another. They both felt haunted by the dark, cold responsibility, and fled hand in hand towards the land of innocence.

# CHAPTER IV

THE spring was early this year, and when Pastor Borring went up the avenue to Norby Farm at the beginning of May, the trees were in leaf, and a strong scent of leaves and grass filled the air. The priest carried a bag in his hand. He was going on a sick visit to Lars Kleven up on the hill.

Many of the young trees in the avenue were torn up or broken off, as if after a hurricane; but it was after the working men's procession to Norby on the first of May.

When the priest came to the garden, he saw Norby inside the fence in a white working coat, busy with some trees. The priest stopped and fell into conversation with him.

"It looks dreadful after the demonstrators," said he with a shake of the head. "Upon my word, it's not only the consul's standing drinks that has fooled them; there must have been some one or other who has dealt out mental strong drinks too."

Norby looked surprised, but laughed as he leaned upon his spade. "The workmen?" he said. "They had nothing to do with the damage in the grounds. The wind did that one night."

The priest looked a little sheepish, and soon went on his way. That Norby had a peculiar way of being proud! He was so terribly afraid that any one should pity him.

The path up the hill was muddy after the rain in the night, but the leaves of the trees and the green slopes were glistening in the sun. Brooks ran noisily towards the fjord, and in the fields round about men and horses were busy harrowing.

At last the priest had mounted the last hill, on which stood the little cottage. Dwelling-house and cow-shed together formed one building; it would be difficult to know the one from the other, were it not for the porch at one end, and two small windows at each side. The steps were washed and the stones strewn with fir twigs, because the priest was expected.

He had to stoop to enter. The ceiling was low, too, so that he had to keep his head bent. A saucepan of water was steaming on the fire, the floor was white and strewn with fir twigs, the wife was sitting dressed in her best with a hymn-book in her hand, and in bed, beneath an old skin coverlet, lay Lars Kleven, in a shirt so white that it must have been put on at the moment the priest was seen at the bottom of the hill. The priest first shook hands with the wife, and then went to the bed.

"And how are you, my dear Lars?"

Lars said nothing, pressed his lips together, and looked at the priest. It was his wife who answered.

"Oh, mercy! How frightened I was that he'd be gone before the priest came!"

The priest took the old man's hand. It was as hard as horn, and quite cold. The furrowed, weather-beaten face was motionless, and the old eyes looked up dully. Now and then his mouth moved, for he still had his quid to chew. The pastor sat down.

"Are you afraid to die, my dear Lars?"

It was again the wife that answered.

"He has something to confess to you," she said.

"Indeed?" The priest looked kindly at the old man in the bed.

The dying man suddenly surprised him by sending a squirt of tobacco-juice out of his mouth on to the floor. "It was about the inquiry," he then said, looking anxiously at the priest.

"Oh! Between Wangen and Norby?"

"He wanted to go and give evidence," said the wife; "but he hadn't the courage to give evidence against Norby."

The priest looked expectantly at Lars, who kept his eyes all the time anxiously on him, still chewing his quid.

"Do you think there's pardon for me?" he asked at length.

"Yes. Why not?" The priest smiled.

"When I didn't go and give evidence to the truth, even though God told me to?"

"Are you sure you knew the truth then, Lars?"

"He went with Norby to town that time when he signed the paper," said the wife, who now stood by the table with her hymn-book in front of her, looking anxiously at the priest.

Pastor Borring sat looking at the floor for a little while.

"And now he thinks there's no pardon for him," said the wife, wiping her eyes. "But I tell him that Christ died for that sin too?"

The priest still looked down at the floor, but he felt the eyes of the dying man eagerly fixed upon him, and he knew that he must answer when he met those eyes.

If Pastor Borring had been alone and uninfluenced by the moment, he would have answered: "Even if Christ died for your sins, and even if you get to heaven, Wangen may suffer just as much in consequence of your sin." He had it in his mind to say it, too, but it was another matter to look up and meet the old, frightened eyes.

"Do you think there's pardon for me?" came at last from the bed; and the priest had to answer.

"Yes," he said looking up.

"Will you pray for me?" said Lars, turning his quid in his mouth. The priest rose and folded his hands; but what should he pray? He thought of Wangen. But the sun shone brightly in upon the fir-strewn floor, throwing a few beams across the old skin coverlet and on the old man's shirt. It was like a message from Him who shines upon the good and the evil, thought the priest, and there was such poverty and helplessness in this little cottage, and the two poor old people filled him with a desire to be merciful, and he began to pray God to be merciful.

When he ended, the wife was crying, and the old man lay with his hands folded upon the coverlet, and the tears running down his cheeks. When the priest sat down, he said: "Will you give me the sacrament?"

The priest rose mechanically and opened his bag. He heard the swallows flying past the window outside in the sunshine, and the starling that had its nest up under the eaves. It was like another message to tell him that life was greater than man's idea of right and wrong.

When he stood ready in his priest's robes, after pouring the wine into the chalice he had brought with him, he said with bowed head: "Listen, Lars. The trial is next week. Won't you ask your wife to go and give evidence for you? I can confirm what you have now confessed?"

"Oh, yes," said the old man, looking longingly at the chalice. The wife sighed upon her bench, but came up and took the quid out of her husband's mouth, and laid it on the window-sill.

When the priest had given the sacrament, and had packed up his gown again, he sat a little longer by the dying man's bedside. It seemed as if Lars had only kept up in expectation of the sacrament and the forgiveness of his sins, and that he now suddenly began to sink. Once he opened his eyes and turned them upon his wife. She understood him, and took the half-chewed quid from the window-sill and put it into his mouth; and Lars looked at her, as much as to say: "Yes, that was it."

The priest rose, and was taking his departure when the dying man looked once more at the priest and then affectionately at his wife, and whispered: "Oh no! She mustn't be made to go and give evidence, for he'll take the cottage from her if she does."

"Very well," said the priest a little uncertainly, as he paused.

Old Lars smiled with content at finding that every prospect had brightened so wonderfully, both for time and eternity; and he settled himself deeper into his pillow. He then wanted to raise his head as if to spit, but could not; the tobacco stuck in his throat, and he coughed; and the cough became a dying rattle, and after a moment that too ceased.

His wife stood some time gazing at him, and then went resolutely up and closed his eyes. She then turned to the priest. "Thank God!" she said with emotion. "Now I know that Lars died saved."

On his way homewards with his bag in his hand the priest stopped on the hill, and sitting down on a stone, rested his chin in his hand, and looked out over the parish.

Whenever Pastor Borring had imparted forgiveness of sins he was always unhappy; for in the first place he did not feel that God had charged him with the forgiveness of sins, and in the second he did not believe in the notion of forgiveness. And yet in the course of time he had laid his hand in church upon the heads of thousands, and lied this dangerous comfort into their souls.

And now he was sitting here, unhappy once more. He had never felt more distinctly than now how altogether meaningless it was to pardon, to forgive. If God forgave Lars Kleven, was He also to pardon on Wangen's behalf? Wangen would perhaps be unjustly condemned, in spite of the pardon. And Wangen's family, who were the sufferers?

No, a wicked action is a thing that is set in motion, and perhaps never stops. It appears in consequences and the consequences of those consequences; it spreads like an infectious disease, and no one knows when or how it will cease. Even if it is lost to sight, it still goes on its way. Who will pardon here? God? Is it His duty to pardon it on the behalf of innocent persons?

Thus thought Pastor Borring as he sat. On his way home he felt saddened and ashamed, as he so often did during the performance of an act from which he did not feel strong enough to free himself.

But what was he to do now? The confessions of a dying man are sacred.

# CHAPTER V

FRU WANGEN had been impatient for the demonstration to take place. The means that she had despised in her husband, she herself now felt a sudden desire to resort to, like a person in despair, who gropes about for anything he can lay hands on.

But after the day when the consul had secretly made the demonstrators drunk, so that they frightened the whole district with their behaviour, both Wangen and his wife saw that these allies of theirs had once more injured their cause; for the whole district was quite sure that Wangen was at the back of it all, and even Norby's worst enemies began to feel sympathy for him and to turn from Wangen.

As the trial approached, Wangen's fear of being left to stand alone became greater and greater. It was witnesses that he must have, and now he no longer relied upon witnesses, for he had a suspicion that every one hated him.

At night, when he lay and polished up his innocence, he saw more and more vividly that scene at the Grand, when the document was signed. At first he had not been quite sure that it was there; but as he had said it once, it was most probable; and the oftener he said it, the more certain he became that it was there and nowhere else. He now even remembered the corner they had sat in. There were Norby, Haarstad and himself, and they were drinking coffee after dinner. But was there no one else? Suppose there had been some one else who had seen it all!

He conjured up this scene more and more vividly, as if it had some hidden power that might suddenly make its appearance and be his salvation. He seemed to sit there, and even to feel the taste of the strong coffee. He saw people at the neighbouring tables, while Norby signed. The cigar-smoke lay in layers in the air, the waiters ran about with napkins under their arms, counted money, and drew corks. Glasses jingled, people laughed and made a noise, and conversation filled the café. And here sat the three, and signed their names. But was there actually no fourth man?

He began to have a suspicion that there had been one more, just because he so earnestly wished it. But perhaps they had bought him too. This thought angered him. It should be brought to light. He went on seeing the hands writing, and the people round looking on. He even saw it when he slept; he saw it when he fixed his eyes upon any one he was speaking to. This was the scene that had to be proved and it therefore appeared in a feverish light, the more helpless he felt himself. At last he really began to have a consciousness that there had actually been a fourth man close by. At first it was only like a shadow on the wall; but the shadow acquired eyes that looked on while Norby signed. It acquired a voice that said: "Yes, I saw it; but I will not interfere in the matter now." Indeed? But he would have to. He should be brought to light, no matter how well he had been paid for not interfering. Wangen became more and more eager to produce him, as the trial pressed closer upon him.

One day he had again met the tailor with the mad eyes, and lay awake at night. He then saw this unknown form more vividly than ever; it resisted and would not advance, but it would have to, by Jove it would! And although Wangen again and again felt impelled to cuff himself and say that he was mad, he could not but wish, hope and cling to this new possibility, which would perhaps save him at the last moment.

One day he told his wife about it, and she became excited and encouraged him almost fiercely. As she questioned him more closely, and he had to answer with probable reasons, it came to be some one whom he did not yet quite recollect: it was several years ago. But to sit and talk about this person became a strengthening draught to them both. At last one evening, when they had once more been sitting and talking about it, and Wangen had been burrowing for some time in his memory, he suddenly sprang up, crying: "I have him!"

"Henry!" exclaimed his wife with a little cry, also rising.

"It was Rasmus Brodersen."

"Oh, thank God!" she panted, with her hands upon her breast. But Rasmus Brodersen was in America. Wangen believed, however, that one of the letters from him was on this subject.

He got out his packets of letters, and began to read through all letters from this old school-friend of his. He did not find it that evening. It was possible it might have been lost.

The excitement and tension of these hours made Fru Wangen quite ill. She wanted to sit up at night, but he wanted to wait until the following day; and as he seated himself with fresh packets of letters the next morning, he thought: "She'll be beside herself if I don't find anything to-day."

At about dinner-time she came in to him in the bedroom where he was sitting, and asked for the twentieth time! "Well?"

"There should still be another packet somewhere or other," he said, scratching his head; and he began to rummage every receptacle to find it.

"It must be in this last packet!" she thought; and she determined to leave him in peace, and let him come himself and tell her. And while she waited for this salvation for them both, she suddenly regained her pride and peace of mind. She went on her errands up to the farm, tall, with slow steps, bare-headed in the sun, her hair like a crown above the pale, beautiful face. Perhaps after all her husband's enemies would be disappointed.

That day was the first on which she had not thought: "I wonder how little Bias is now!" And as regarded her father—it was a great trouble and sorrow, but it no longer caused a bad conscience.

At dinner-time she went and listened at his door. She heard the rustling of paper, but she dared not disturb him to say that dinner was ready, although she had got some unusually good meat to-day, that she knew he would like.

At last he came out, quite pleased and satisfied. He had not found it yet, but he was so sure that he would have it before the evening. The decided promise nearly turned her head with joy. Sleepless nights and emotion had unhinged her, and while they dined she was childishly gay. Oh no, he should be let off having to tell her, if only it came to light that evening; and she drank to his health in water, and put her finger in his glass to change his water into wine for him; and while she laughed over this, the tears stood in her eyes.

She was on thorns all the afternoon; but he had asked to be left alone, and he should be.

At last he opened the door, and said, smiling: "Here it is, Karen!"

Once more she started up with the cry of "Henry!" Then she ran to him, seized the paper from him, and began to run through it. Ah, yes! It was written a couple of years ago, and mentioned a good dinner, and further on—yes, there it was! There it was!

She hung upon his neck, took his head between her hands and held it from her while she murmured: "Why don't you kiss me? Why don't you fly up to the ceiling? Oh, I shall faint!" She had to take the paper to read it once more. But—but—a cold shiver suddenly ran through her. This handwriting—it—it was so suspiciously like Wangen's own. She looked quickly up at him, but she dared not say anything.

"When I produce this in court," he said, smiling, "I think it will be enough."

"Yes, of course, Henry." She still laughed with delight, but was obliged to sit down. "What has he done?" she thought, sitting and gazing straight before her. "God help me!" Everything seemed to crumble to pieces, and she gazed into his guilt in everything, in everything! But this could not be! It must not, must not be! She might have made a mistake. She would not look at the letter any more, and she gave it back to him with a smile, and begged him to take good care of it. It might perhaps help him a little, only a little; for he must be let off.

That evening, when they were in bed, she said: "You don't write any more in the papers now, Henry, but I think it might very well come to the knowledge of the public how the pastor and Thora have behaved to us."

"Yes," he said; "and it might be a good thing if it were read by the jurymen, too, before they went to pass verdict on me."

And they tried to sleep, with hands interclasped.

# CHAPTER VI

A MAN was coming down the hills from the north, and stopped at Norby Sæter, at the door of which Einar was sitting making a birch-broom.

While the stranger lay full length upon the grass, his head resting on his wallet, he related how he had met a she-bear and two cubs west of the Great Snow-field. As news from the valley, he mentioned that Wangen's trial was to take place that day.

"Indeed?" said Einar, and went on with his birch-broom.

He rowed the man across the mountain lake, for he was going west and down into the other valley. Einar heard that the doctor's twenty-year-old daughter had come up to Buvik Sæter, and this awakened pleasant recollections of the ball at Christmas.

He had lived here for a month in delightful quiet. For company he had the old dairymaid, the dog and the cattle. He was to drink milk, go for walks, keep his feet dry, and sleep and eat well. And day after day he plodded about in wooden shoes and frieze clothes like any peasant. It was splendid!

But now his peace was destroyed. The news of the trial had cut like a knife. Old wounds were reopened, and he felt a despair approaching, which he was not equal to bearing, and to which he involuntarily rose in opposition, in order to dismiss it. Had he not suffered enough in this matter?

At night, when he lay sleepless, he represented to himself how good his father had always been; but as that did not feel sufficient, he resorted to the young girl who was also up in the mountains now at a sæter. How pretty she had been last Christmas when they danced together! People whispered and pointed at them. But why had he thought so little about her since? "I'm too old-fashioned," he thought; "I live in books and great ideas, and meanwhile the good years are passing, and I haven't lived the life of youth. But there is sunshine in the world, too, thank goodness."

These thoughts helped him to make the young girl's stay in the mountains still more important, and at length he fell asleep in the middle of a dance with her, just as at Christmas.

The day following, when he went for a walk over the hill, he frequently stopped to look at Buvik Sæter. It lay on the other side of the lake just below the snow-field, at a distance of some three or four miles. "Perhaps he's already in prison" was the thought that cut through him; but he still looked up oftener and oftener towards Buvik Sæter, which had now acquired much greater importance than before. Smoke was rising from the little grey houses; perhaps she was preparing her dinner.

As the days passed, his thoughts were continually occupied with the young girl, as he then had no time to think of anything unpleasant or painful. He was no longer alone; there were he and she, they two alone in the mountains. Two eyes always seemed to be resting on him from something beautiful close by. They were so near one another, because they were many miles from the valley. He might go there on a visit, but he would prefer that they should meet by chance, perhaps down on the lake.

He often fished along the shore on the other side, but he never saw her; and when he rowed home he laughed at himself for actually being disappointed and sad.

He had to keep her continually in his thoughts in order to feel quite calm. The mountains seemed to acquire a peculiar grandeur. One evening he rowed out to a little island, and lighted a large bonfire; but still no boat came rowing out; only the silent shores looked on. He no longer went about in wooden shoes, however; and he always took care that his shirt and his hands were clean. Not because he expected any one, but because there was always something beautiful within him, for which he had to adorn himself.

At last one day a man came up from the valley with a pack-horse, and before Einar could prevent him, he had told him that Wangen was sentenced to a year's hard labour. The punishment had been increased, because he had produced a forged letter in court.

Einar sat on the doorstep and heard this. He covered his face with his hands, and sat motionless.

"And I think of going on with my studies! I, who can never look any one in the face again!"

It was a beautiful day, with a clear sky above the brown moors and distant blue mountain ridges, and the snow-fields lay shining like silver in the sun.

In the evening Einar went down to the lake and pushed off the boat. He had thought for a time that the whole world was extinguished, and that he ought to jump into the water because he was too full of shame to live. But from force of habit he once more recalled the young girl to his mind; and just because he himself now stood so immeasurably low, it seemed to him that she stood high—high, and stretched out her hands to rescue him. He rowed slowly over the smooth water, in the middle of which the red sky was reflected. Twilight enveloped the silent shores in a light haze. The houses and the green fold of Norby Sæter were reflected in the water, and in the wake of the boat lay two rows of rings in the water, left by the dip of his oars.

Gradually he seemed to enter a peaceful land, and at last he shipped the oars, and let the boat drift. Gradually the world grew large and radiant. The moors looked at him and smiled. Everybody was happy in the main.

"Good heavens!" he thought. "Now I'm beginning to understand what love is."

# CHAPTER VII

ONE Saturday afternoon, Thora of Lidarende went out towards the Sound. It was in hay-making time, and the mowers were on the hills, making the hay into cocks for the evening. The fresh scent of hay was wafted through the air. Lake Mjösen lay still and clear, so that Fru Thora could see the stony bottom a long way out.

She turned up the avenue to the big parish school building, entered the yard, and hastened up the steps, for there were others she must manage to call on to-day.

Although the principal was occupied for the time being with some pupils in dialect, his wife went and fetched him when she heard that Fru Thora had come on an important errand; and soon they were all three sitting round a table in the large, comfortable drawing-room, with port wine in front of them.

Principal Heggen was a man of about fifty years of age, with a bald head, a long brown beard, and spectacles. He had a fine, high forehead, and nice eyes. He was well known for his kind disposition, and as he was most unsuspecting, he loved many things. As regarded religion, he was a warm advocate of a national Christianity.

"Yes, I've come on an important errand to-day," said Fru Thora, sipping her glass.

Both the schoolmaster and his wife looked attentively at her. She continued with a smile as she looked from the one to the other:

"It's in connection with recent events. It has been a sad time, and a disgrace to the district."

"Yes," said Fru Heggen, shaking her head as she knitted.

"But we who sit here have got off fairly well. I only got sneered at a little in the papers because I was rude enough to wish to take one of their children for a time; and you, Heggen, have been found fault with because you remained neutral." Fru Thora could not help laughing.

"Poor man!" said the schoolmaster, playing with his beard.

"Ye-es! It's hard on him, and we won't judge Wangen," said she, "but as long as we live in an orderly community, I suppose we have the right to some protection; and it doesn't do to go on as Wangen has done."

Fru Heggen shook her head once more, said "No," and looked at her husband.

"But the person who has suffered most during this time, dear friends, is Norby; and I've come to propose that we make him some reparation in one form or another."

Heggen rose, and left the table in order to fill himself a pipe, which he slowly lighted, and then returned to the table and seated himself. Out of doors the sun was beginning to set, and sent golden beams in to them through the tree-tops in the garden.

"Well, what did you think of doing?" Heggen finally asked, while he endeavoured to make his pipe draw.

Fru Thora coloured a little. She had expected that she would meet with opposition here, so she had come here first. She braced herself, and continued courageously:

"Well, we see what our great politicians, for instance, do when one of their number has been exposed to unjust attacks. They give him a banquet. And I think we might give a little festive entertainment for Norby; it might be as simple as possible."

Heggen and his wife looked at one another.

"Ye-es," said he; but with a slightly embarrassed smile.

There was a short pause, which Fru Thora dared not allow to become too long.

"With reference to the heart of the matter," she said, "you, too, believe, do you not, that Norby was altogether in the right?"

"Yes," said Heggen, shaking his head a little. There seemed to be something he would not say.

"Yes," said Fru Heggen, too; "he's said from the very first that Wangen was guilty, and Heggen has a wonderful power of judgment in such cases."

"Well, then," said Fru Thora, "I hope you won't let old disagreements stand in the way this time. We ought really to begin to appreciate the worth of others than those we always agree with."

"Oh dear yes!" said Heggen eagerly. "But who did you think of asking to join?"

Fru Thora laid her pretty hand upon the table, as if to give more emphasis to her words.

"All who wish to. The authorities, peasants—all without difference. Wouldn't it be nice if government officers and country people for once joined hands and said: 'One of our best men has been persecuted, and his name sullied; here we are, and we will join hands and wash him clean again.' An example should really be set to show that Christianity and national feeling are not mere words, but that we actually help a brother when he is in need."

"Has Norby taken it to heart?" asked Heggen, with a look of sympathy.

"I don't know; he is so proud, that man. He certainly doesn't complain. But now, to-day, my brother in Bergen wrote to me and asked if it were really true that Norby had defrauded the widow for whom he's trustee! That's the way ill-natured remarks spread; and how much wouldn't a man lose by such things!"

"Oh yes," sighed Fru Heggen; "there's always some one ready to repeat an ill-natured thing."

"And there's one thing we must be all agreed about," continued Fru Thora, "and that is that a better head of a family and master than Norby is not to be found in the district. Where will you find any one so good to his old servants and men?"

The schoolmaster thought it over, and the warm appreciation of Norby's goodness to his farm-servants touched him and overcame his last scruples.

"Well, I'm quite willing to join," he said. "But who is to make the speech?" he thought to himself.

"Yes," said Fru Thora, taking another sip of wine. "But you aren't going to be let off so easily. You will have to make the speech. No one can do it so well."

"I?" said Heggen, his brow flushing; but he finally agreed. If a few words were to be said in honour of Fru Norby, perhaps Fru Thora of Lidarende might attempt them.

When she left, she felt relieved and happy at having succeeded here. Now the rest would be easily managed; and she hastened down the avenue as briskly as a young girl, while the last rays of the sun fell through the leaves upon her light dress.

With no suspicion of Fru Thora's plan, Knut Norby was sitting that day hard at work with his accounts. He had at last fallen again into his old ways. He had wasted so much time on all that nonsense with Wangen that there must be an end of this; he must set to work and make up for what he had lost.

His hair had grown a little greyer during the last few months, and he was pale and tired; it had been rather trying, the way things had gone on.

When he had finished and gone out on to the steps with his pipe in his mouth, Ingeborg came up to him, and told him, with tears in his eyes, that the old dairymaid was dead.

Norby put his pipe in his waistcoat pocket and went across with her to the little cottage. The two old farm men were sitting by the bed in the little room, looking straight before them, with their large coarse hands folded between their knees. The eyes of the one who had been engaged over and over again to the dairymaid were wet.

Norby, too, stood and looked at the old dead servant with trembling lips.

That afternoon he went up over the hills to the little cottage where Lars Kleven's widow sat sorrowful. When he entered—he had to stoop under the ceiling—the old woman was sitting by her spinning-wheel. She rose in alarm, thinking, "He's come to take the cottage from me after all."

"How are you?" asked Norby, sitting down with his stick between his knees.

"Thank God, I can't complain of my health," she said timidly, "but I'm dreading the winter."

"Well, the dairymaid's leaving us now," said the old man, "and her little room will be empty. If you can be satisfied with it, you can move into it for the rest of your days. I think they clean it to-day, so it'll be ready to-morrow. And your cow and fowls—yes—you can bring them with you. There's room enough."

The old woman folded her hands and gazed at him in amazement for a little while, before she sank down and burst into tears. But at that Norby left; he did not like tears.

As he trudged homewards he had no feeling of having done anything good; he had only moved a thing into its proper place. It is true her husband had let himself be tempted by Wangen and his people, but he, poor fellow, lay in his grave now, and there was nothing more to be said about that.

On the hill he sat down and looked out over the valley, which lay bathed in the last gleams of sunshine, with long, blue shadows over the lake. He sat there for some time, his hands resting upon his stick.

He felt as if he had come into a haven after a long storm. They had been evil days and sleepless nights; but one could not expect to have things always go well. They had tried every possible way to injure him—lies and slander, newspaper vulgarity, riots at his farm, and—influencing Einar. Well, well, the boy should never hear the slightest allusion to that matter.

But there was one thing that the old man could hardly help laughing at, and that was that at one time he had really thought that his own hands were not quite clean. He smiled now and shook his head; it was too funny. He remembered, too, now, that at that dinner in town Wangen had asked him to stand surety. But that they had then gone to the Grand and signed——? It was incredible audacity to say such a thing!

It was what his wife always said—he was often too kind-hearted, especially in good company; and because he was kind-hearted, he had believed that if Wangen could go and say he had stood surety there must be something in it. He did not know then what a scoundrel the fellow was.

And now at last there would be peace in the district again, and labour conditions would be decent once more. Perhaps some people believed some of the calumnies about him. Well, let them believe them! He lived on his farm, and cared for no one.

But it was hard on Wangen's wife. They said she had taken to her bed after the trial.

When Norby got home he found Fru Thora of Lidarende in the drawing-room. She had come to say that half the district, with the authorities at their head, had subscribed to a dinner in his honour.

"Nonsense!" he said, laughing; for at first he would not believe it at all, but when she asked what day would suit him, he sighed and considered. It must be true then.

In a little while he answered: "Well—I can't go to any sort of entertainment as long as some one is lying dead here."

Marit Norby looked at him in surprise, but understood at once that it would be useless to dispute the matter.

When Fru Thora went away she was almost disappointed because the old man had not been more touched by the dinner. "It's possible to be too proud," she thought.

# CHAPTER VIII

WHEN at length the day for the dinner could be fixed, it became a busy time for Fru Thora. She managed to get it agreed to, that for once they should try to kindle exhilaration without the aid of strong drink; there should be only home-made wine and milk. To make up for this, she got hold of the best members of the young men's club, and began to rehearse a play that was to be acted after the dinner. She also intended to decorate the walls of the large town-hall, in which the dinner was to be held, in a way that would form a suitable frame to the guest of honour.

When at last the great day arrived she was both worn-out and nervous; for, as usual when one person is energetic and throws himself heart and soul into a matter, the other members of the dinner-committee had sat down and left everything to her.

In the afternoon of that day she heard that Fru Wangen was still confined to her bed; whereupon Fru Thora very quickly made up her mind that she could not take part in any gaiety that evening without first having inquired about the poor woman. If there was nothing else to be done, she would offer to take her in for a time, and the children with her.

When she came to the little cottage among the fir-trees in which the Wangens had last lived, she found the door locked and the shutters before the windows. An uncomfortable fear made her actually run up to the farm, where she met a girl who was drawing up water from a well.

"Where is Fru Wangen?" she asked.

"She is up in an attic here," said the girl.

"I suppose I can go up to her?"

The girl shook her head. Fru Wangen would not even speak to the master; and both the priest and the doctor had come to see her, and she would not see either of them.

"Oh, but do go up and tell her it's me!" said Fru Thora.

The girl took the bucket and went; but when she came out on to the steps again, she shook her head. Fru Wangen wanted to be alone. Besides, the girl then added, she had got up and was going to see her children.

"But what is she going to do now?" asked Fru Thora.

"Nobody knows," said the girl. "She doesn't say a word about it."

Fru Thora had tears in her eyes as she went homewards. Of course this dinner for Norby must wound Fru Wangen, but it really could not be helped. Guilt is guilt, and reparation must be made to the innocent.

It was Saturday afternoon, and the dinner was at seven. The last loads of hay had been driven in from the fields, and the well-raked hills had taken on a soft, dark green colour; while the leafy slopes had here and there begun to get golden patches, upon which the sun shone.

When, at about six o'clock, the first carriages drove up towards the town-hall, they met near the fjord a tall, pale woman, hurrying along with bent head. It was Fru Wangen. Her little, faded straw hat seemed to have been put on in a hurry, and stood off too much from her head, raised by the quantity of fair hair that still lay like a crown above her pale beautiful face.

When she got out to the ridge that descends steeply to the fjord, she saw no more carriages in front of her, and seated herself upon a stone by the wayside. She rested her elbows on her knees, and her chin in her hands, and gazed out over the fjord whose calm surface reflected the red clouds in the sky.

When she had seen the children, where should she go?—what should she do? Could she keep both herself and them? Or—Oh no, she ought not to think of that now; for thinking was what she could not and dared not do. She passed her hand across her forehead and sighed. "I must take care," she thought, "that what is in there doesn't get loose, for then I might go mad; and then I shouldn't be allowed even to see the children."

She had had a letter from Wangen that day; he said that he was trying to obtain a pardon. But she was not equal to further faith; she could not believe in his innocence any more. If he had only confessed it at first, at any rate to her! But now! Her father had been right. Her father! The whole thing overwhelmed her like a terrible darkness.

Suddenly she started up and hurried on. She must manage to reach the children before dark, for she dared not be out alone when it was dark.

When the carriage drove down the avenue from Norby Farm, the two daughters sat opposite their parents, and Einar with the coachman on the box. Einar had come home quite unexpectedly. That evening when he rowed across to Buvik Sæter he had met with a great disappointment. The doctor's daughter had left for the valley that afternoon.

From that time Einar found it unbearable up on the mountains. It was no help now, in his expeditions over the moors, to look over to Buvik Sæter. The disgrace he had fled from now met him both out of doors and indoors; and his eagerness to reach this young woman thereby became greater than ever. So he packed up his things and set off. He must catch her up; he must know for a certainty whether she cared for him or not.

At home he settled down in a wonderful way. The good conscience that every one there had was infectious; and he could not but feel glad that his parents should now be rewarded for all their troubles with this dinner. It was high time that he, too, gave up his ugly suspicion.

As he sat upon the box, he gazed at the carriages that were driving up to the flag-decorated town-hall. Would she be there this evening?

Marit Norby looked handsome as she sat leaning a little towards her husband, dressed in a silk dress and light straw bonnet. Knut, however, was by no means happy; for as he grew to feel himself more and more firmly in the right, he had become more indifferent to the respect of the district. Fancy if people were making this fuss because they were sorry for him! In that case he would like to tell them that they were mistaken. There was nothing the matter with him yet. Nevertheless as he saw carriage after carriage drive up to the town-hall a smile played about the corners of his mouth; for he was thinking of Mads Herlufsen. Would he come? Or was he sitting at home sulking? In that case Norby would like to see him.

As they drove into the yard of the town-hall, Einar saw the doctor's gig driving away. There was room for only two in it, the doctor and his wife, so *she* was not there. He had been so anxious about this for days and nights past that the disappointment was very great, and for a moment he lost all desire to go in. Something awoke in him, that shook him and said: "What are you about, Einar?"

Between two flags on the steps stood the bailiff and Fru Thora of Lidarende to receive the guests of honour; and Einar slowly followed the others up the steps.

Laura, who to-day was wearing her first light silk dress, grew suddenly red when she noticed a beardless youth standing in the passage and looking at her. It was the bailiff's son, who had just taken his degree in forestry. "I wonder if he will take me in to dinner!" she thought, her heart beginning to beat.

The only person who lived in the town-hall building was the midwife of the district, who had two rooms in one wing. There the pastor's wife was now busy, at the head of a flock of maids, serving the dinner. She was both angry and in despair, because the Railway Hotel, which was providing the dinner, had forgotten to send gravy with the joint, and now a servant came and said that Norby had come, and that people were sitting down to table.

"Who's asked them to sit down to table?" cried the pastor's wife. "A nice dinner-committee they are!" And she rushed to the telephone and rang up violently. "Hullo! Are you never going to let us have that gravy?"

# CHAPTER IX

WHEN Norby entered the hall, the first thing he noticed was that Herlufsen was not among the guests; but all the other magnates were there, and there was a general greeting when he appeared.

It was a large, airy hall, and the setting sun shone through the long windows that looked out upon the fjord, and formed three broad bands of light across the floor, upon which the festively attired guests moved, either through the dark or through the gold. There was a hum of conversation, and there was a continual cracking of whips outside, where fresh carriages were driving up to the steps, or off towards the roads.

Among the dress-coated farmers, who cautiously kept close to the walls, while they glanced at the long table decorated with flowers, strutted the owner of the saw-mills, a stout man, with a gold chain dangling upon his expansive waistcoat. He laughed loudly, and his red face shone; for when he had heard that there was nothing to be got here but home-made wine, he had indulged a little before he left home. "Ladies and gentlemen," he said, with a wave of his hand, "I don't think you're in a properly festive mood yet."

The magistrate, a stout man with silvery hair and beard, took Norby by the arm and pointed out the walls. They were decorated with flags and garlands of leaves; and here and there, in place of arms, were old, artistic, domestic articles, such as painted and carved harness and saddles, wooden spoons and bowls with flowers painted on them. Fru Thora had lent the rudiments of her country museum.

"Look here!" said the magistrate, with a pleasant little laugh. "Isn't that pretty? There's Norwegian nature in the greenery, freedom in the flags, and our northern culture in all the rest. The combination forms a beautiful harmony."

"Yes, it's quite pretty," said Norby, with a slight yawn. Suddenly he felt his coat-tails pulled, and turning round he found two old acquaintances smiling at him, both farmers from up the valley, who had been jurymen at the trial.

"What, have you come all this way?" said Norby, taking them by the hand.

They told him that Wangen was supposed to be busy upon a fresh newspaper article, which accused the jurymen of partiality, and when they heard that, they were so angry that—that they set their teeth, and came to the dinner too.

But now Norby was led to the table. At one end of the long table a kind of raised seat had been arranged for the guest of honour; and on one side of him sat his wife, on the other the wife of the magistrate. When he looked down the table, and all the handsome women in gay silk bodices, and male notorieties with wide shirt-fronts, he could not help turning his head to his wife and whispering: "This is just like what we had at our silver wedding."

During the soup, Einar got into a discussion with a member of the Storthing, who sat opposite him. Several others took part in the discussion, and Einar grew angry, but suddenly he felt as if an invisible hand had struck him, and a voice within him said: "Yes, be severe in your judgment of others, Einar, you who are such a hero yourself!" And he instantly bowed his head and was silent; and he felt the blood mount to his face.

Laura, true enough, had been paired with the bailiff's son; and though he had not yet noticed her new dress, she still felt that everything was wrapped in a wonderful golden mist, and she had a vague notion that this was her own wedding.

"After dinner you must help me with something," he said to her.

"What is it?" she asked curiously, as she tried to push an obstinate wave of hair off her forehead.

"I won't tell you now. You must wait."

When the joint was served, the schoolmaster rose and tapped his glass. This was Fru Thora's great moment, and she felt her heart beat with joy and pride, for there had been so much ill-will between the schoolmaster Heggen and Knut Norby. Now Heggen was standing there, and was going to make a speech in honour of his enemy. This was her work. And there had been many misunderstandings between the schoolmaster and the old magistrate; but she had made Heggen take the magistrate's daughter in to dinner; for they should all be friends this evening, and learn to understand one another.

Looking at the speaker, "Isn't he handsome?" she whispered to the gentleman who had taken her in. The sun was just sinking, and its last rays played upon the glass on the table, and made the tulips in the large bouquets glow.

Forks were laid down and faces turned towards the schoolmaster's tall figure. His voice vibrated with emotion, and Fru Thora thought she had never heard him speak so beautifully as now when he was making a speech in honour of his old enemy. He called this dinner an event in the district. He held his glass in one hand, and with the other fingered his long beard, and looked at nothing in particular through his spectacles, while the sun threw a ray of light across his fine forehead.

This was an event, because he had never seen so many dissimilar people united in a common object, a common desire to do good. There were still Birkebeins and Baglers to divide people in this country; but this evening he seemed to read a message of spring in this festive meeting. Like Olaf at Stiklestad, he seemed to be looking out over the whole country with its blue hills and shining fjords, over farms and lands, and into the many minds; and he descried the day when all men would be united in a sabbath atmosphere, with hands joined in brotherhood, united in waging war against the powers of evil, united in helping those who had suffered wrong. "Whatever religion we profess, or party we belong to, we shall henceforward agree in considering that the human in man is higher than all difference of opinion; and when the human being, Norby, suffers persecution and derogation, as he has lately done, we hasten to him, enclose him in a chain of fraternity, and say: 'Here are we, your brothers and sisters, Knut Norby; we will wash you clean. Here we are!'"

Scarcely a breath was heard during the impressive speech, until the sound of gentle weeping was heard a little way up the table. It was Fru Heggen, who always cried when her husband made a speech.

Gradually several faces turned from the speaker to the guests of the evening. Fru Norby sat with her eyes full of tears, and smiled; but Norby looked down, and modestly shook his head, as if to say, "You mustn't say anything more, Heggen."

When at length the speech came to an end, and the guests rose to drink with the guests of honour, the saw-mill owner roared: "Long live Norby and Fru Norby! Hip, hip!" And his abandonment to the spirit of the occasion was quickly followed, and the hurrahs rang.

Ingeborg sat and looked on with tears in her eyes. Her joy was unbounded, she thought how patiently her father had borne all the persecution; she thought of her prayers, and involuntarily looked upwards, saying to herself: "My God, I thank Thee for answering my prayers." She seemed to see a host of good, protecting spirits, above the heads of her parents up there. Her mother looked at her; they both had tears in their eyes and smiled. They remembered the night when they dared not go to bed after the riots at Norby.

To Marit Norby it seemed now as if all evil, all suspicion were melting and must be wept out; and it felt so delightful that she could not help smiling all the time.

But worse was to come, when Fru Thora of Lidarende rose, after the knives and forks had clattered for a time, and made a speech in her honour. It was a woman's and a mother's heart beating with hers. Mention was made of her struggle to keep up her husband's courage in adversity, even while she was nursing her son through a dangerous illness. It was a great deed, a woman's heroic action, such as is seldom mentioned at festive entertainments, but is often, very often performed in secret.

No one had ever heard such eloquence in a woman. She stood there, slim, youthful in appearance despite her five and forty years, full of fire and warmth of feeling. Her hearers were astonished that this feeling did not overwhelm her and make her burst into tears; but she stood and smiled all the time, although her eyes were wet. Every one had to acknowledge that she was handsome, in her plain black dress and little white lace collar about her neck. It was no wonder that she showed feeling, for she was thinking all the time of her own son, the little Gunnar of Lidarende, who was in bed with whooping cough.

The toasting and cheers for Fru Norby were deafening; but she burst into audible weeping, for it was true. It had been a hard time.

At the mention of his mother and his illness, Einar was also touched, and went up and drank with his parents.

It had gradually grown so dark that the large hanging lamps over the table had to be lighted; and although there was nothing but home-made wine, spirits had risen, so that most of the faces shone red in the lamplight, the conversation was lively, and the laughter resounded.

The two jurymen were seated at the lower end of the table. One of them now said cautiously to the other: "Isn't it customary to chair the guest of honour?"

"We musn't be in a hurry," said the other as cautiously.

"What was it we called Norby, when we were at the agricultural school with him?"

"Fatty," said the other, surreptitiously taking up a bone in his fingers. His companion began to laugh; for it was so amusing to think that they had once been so intimate with Norby as to call him Fatty.

But now a silence fell on the assembly when Norby himself tapped his glass. He rose, a little red in the face, and looked first at Marit and then at the company assembled. His voice was hoarse when he said: "I must return thanks both for myself and my wife. And now I will ask you to drink to the health of one of whom I cannot help thinking this evening—the judge." And when the health had been drunk, Fru Thora cried enthusiastically: "Long live the judge! Long live the jury!"

This evoked loud applause, and the saw-mill owner led the enthusiasm with his hip, hip. One of the jurymen started up, saying: "Come! Now we'll take him!" "Don't be in a hurry!" said the other. "Yes," said the first. "We'll show people that we repudiate Wangen's charge of partiality!"

At this the other rose, too, and they both stole up to take Norby by the arms. At first the old man resisted strenuously, but when one of the jurymen said: "Come now, Fatty," memories of younger days were called up, and he laughed and gave in. The whole company shouted when he was carried round; and when he had got back to his seat, Fru Thora got up and said to a young farmer's wife: "Then Fru Norby shall be carried round too!" And they rushed up and took Marit by the arms, and the enthusiasm increased, except with the saw-mill owner, where it gradually began to come to a sad end. While the others grew merrier as they ate and drank home-made wine, his spirits began to go down more and more, and he whispered to the magistrate: "Don't you think we shall have a little something with the coffee?"

The magistrate shook his head, and the mill-owner sighed deeply, and wiped his forehead.

"I say," said Norby to his wife; "it's strange that Herlufsen isn't here!"

"How naughty you are!" whispered Marit, laughing; and the old man chuckled.

More speeches followed, the best being one by a young teacher in honour of his country. The national song was then sung standing, several taking parts; and finally Pastor Borring rose. He knew that he was expected to say something, and although his presence had been well considered, he felt strangely oppressed. After Wangen had made use of a forged letter in court, he understood of course that his first supposition had been correct, and that Lars Kleven's confession had only been the crotchet of a dying man; but nevertheless he could not help thinking of Wangen, and to the surprise of every one he now began to speak of him. He asked those present to give a sympathetic thought to the unfortunate man who was guilty. It had been rightly said this evening that they should join hands round him who is innocent. Quite right! But let them also, if only in spirit, at the same time join hands round him who was guilty. He stood most in need of reparation and help. And his wife—; but here the pastor could say no more, and sat down; and there were tears in several eyes.

A fresh astonishment was created when Norby tapped his glass, and rising said: "I propose that we start a list to make a collection for Fru Wangen. I will do what I can myself. We must remember that she is left with three children unprovided for!"

There was a pause when he sat down. People looked at one another with eyes that said "He's a man in a thousand!"

# CHAPTER X

AFTER the sweets came coffee, and the conversation was soon being carried on through clouds of tobacco-smoke.

"Do you know who Norby is like?" said Fru Thora to her neighbour, who was the magistrate.

The magistrate looked up with his cigar in his mouth, and answered: "No—at least, yes——"

"Don't you see he's like Garibaldi?"

"Well, now you say it," said the magistrate.

All down the table the talk was exclusively of Norby. It came naturally. Two farmers told of the King's last journey through the district, when Norby quietly went up and took him by the hand, and bade him welcome to the district. Einar had to tell the bailiff's wife about his grandfather, Ingeborg was questioned about her mother; the magistrate praised the old man for his skill in the game of boston; an estate administrator told about a probate case in which Norby was arbitrator, and how clever he was in bringing people to reason; the doctor sat and talked about the shape of the old man's head, and especially the sign of race in the forehead. There was a buzz of homage in the form of little sympathetic touches unearthed from the memories of all present and held up to view; and at last the old man was raised higher and higher, borne as it were by all that was wept, said, sung, and felt there this evening—elevated upon a golden cloud of sympathy and admiration.

Einar alone had grown coldly serious at the pastor's speech, and various questions thronged in upon him. Through all the rosy clouds that enveloped this table he seemed to get a glimpse into—something different.

The best feelings and ideals of every one seemed to have met this evening to pay homage to his father; and he no longer dared to think whether his father were the guilty one or not. But if— Could it be that the most sacred human feelings and ideals were completely blind, so that they could just as easily lend themselves to glorify a crime, a black lie? Could it be? Surely not! Was it no guarantee when people's words were glowing with the whole warmth of their heart, when their eyes were wet and their voice trembled with emotion? Was that so? Surely not! But if— Was it no excuse to have done a thing in all good faith? For the fact remained that if people crowned the criminal, and threw the innocent into prison, good faith was the most terrible thing of all; for it committed its bad actions with divine good conscience, and every one laid down their arms before it. Was it so? And did all such forces as God, one's country, philanthropy, Christianity, lend themselves as garments to adorn the wrong-doer and honour the lie? No, no! it must not, could not, be so. But that was why there was so much wrong done in the world. The wet eyes, the warm tones, the glowing hearts, always formed a defensive covering for that which was bad. Was it so?

And what about himself? Had not his best feelings for his parents made him a— He dared not think the word.

It must not, it could not, be so! He involuntarily wished there were strong drink in his glass, and that he could drink himself into a happy mood with wine as the others did with their speeches.

He raised his glass, and tried to smile at Ingeborg. She raised hers in return, while she thought, "Thank God that Einar was undeceived!"

Suddenly some one said: "Oh, look out there!" Several rose from the table and went to the windows. Against the dark fjord, that reflected the starry sky, a gleaming rocket rose into the air, while another was already raining down in fiery sparks of many colours. A new one rose, and in its first brilliant blaze Laura could be seen bare-headed and in her silk dress, and by her side the bailiff's son.

There were several exclamations, and Ingeborg said: "Oh indeed! That was why Laura had a headache and had to go out!"

A fresh rocket blazed up and illuminated the two standing in the dark, just as Laura took hold of the young man's arm to draw him a little way from the rocket. It was her first tender care for him. Then it was dark once more about them, while the fiery sparks rained down from the sky, reflected all the time in the dark, still fjord, into which they finally fell.

"Look!" cried those at the windows. "Oh, look!" "Oh, that was lovely!" "Both blue and red!" And all the time momentary flashes of light gleamed upon the two young people, who stood there and sent up bright messengers into the sky in the still evening.

When at last this was over the lamps in the hall were suddenly extinguished. A tittering was heard, and a few indignant ladies' voices; but suddenly a curtain was drawn aside, and revealed a Norwegian mountain landscape illuminated by paraffin lamps.

"Goodness me!" thought Einar. "Are we going to have that old play that everybody knows?"

But all at once a young girl in Norwegian costume came forward and began to talk to an old man. It was—Einar gazed in perplexity—it was she! It was the doctor's young daughter. That was why she had not been at the dinner, then. She had perhaps been rehearsing up to the last moment.

Sore and despondent and disturbed as Einar was already, this surprise threw him into the greatest agitation. His heart beat, and something warm began to run through his limbs. There she was! And how lovely she was in that dress! And gradually the oil-lamps turned into sunshine, and the ridiculous decorations into actual wood and mountain; and the good patriotic moral of the play acted upon him with a wonderful power.

But when the young girl went off the stage the piece seemed to lose its interest, and he turned to Fru Thora with the question whether there was to be dancing afterwards. "Yes," she said. Good! He would ask the doctor whether his daughter might stay, if he promised to see her home. Perhaps it might turn out a wonderful evening for him yet.

# CHAPTER XI

KNUT NORBY drove home through the still night with Marit and Ingeborg, as the other two stayed on for the dancing. A golden moon had risen above the hills in the east, and shone upon the waving corn-fields and the calm fjord. It was such good weather just now for the crops that it promised to be a good harvest; and as Knut sat there he was filled with a gentle peace, and felt a desire to thank God.

As they passed the churchyard, he looked in involuntarily. Who could tell how soon he might be lying there? It was better to make good use of the time while one had it. Lars Kleven lay there now—he who so wanted to lie quiet in his grave. Well, God grant he might have peace! And there lay the dairy-maid in her freshly-made grave, and was perhaps dreaming now in the early morning that she had to get up to go to the cows.

A warm wind sighed on the leafy slopes, and brought a scent of fermenting hay from the lofts about. Mountain and lake lay in a great calm peace.

"Thank God!" said Ingeborg, looking up at the stars; and they all three sat with the same feeling, and words were unnecessary.

When at length they drove into the yard, Knut saw that the flag was still up; the servants had forgotten to take it down. But Norby did not get angry now; he could take it down himself.

When he called for some one to take the horse, no one came.

"Have they all gone to bed?" said Marit, a little out of humour.

"Oh well," said Norby, "it's not much to be wondered at; they have to be up in the morning." And he began to unharness the horse himself.

When at length he came up to the bedroom, Marit already lay yawning in bed, but Norby began to pace up and down the floor, with his thumbs hooked into the armholes of his waistcoat. He was in far too good humour to go to bed at once.

"Ah well," said Marit quietly, "this can be an example to others, and encourage people to be patient and enduring."

"Yes," said Norby, stopping at the window, where he could see the fjord in the moonlight, "the main thing is to act honourably and uprightly." In a little while he said: "I don't know how it is, but I seem to have been away from Norby for a long time, and only to have properly come home again now."

"Dear me, yes!" yawned Marit. "But it has been a hard time."

Norby still looked out over the lake in the moonlight. "There must have been some purpose in it all," he said. "I may often have acted with too great severity, but now I think it will be better for every one in the district. I shall do my part, at any rate."

His wife did not answer: presumably she was too tired.

When at last Norby got into bed, he folded his hands and said a couple of verses of a hymn. He felt so near to God; and the respect and sympathy of the whole district now shone into his conscience, but he would thank God for it all.

"But there is one thing I can't understand," he thought after a while, "and that is how people can stand like Wangen with a calm face and lie in court. God help those who have no more conscience than to do it!"